Fake Marrying the Billionaire

Elizabeth Lynx

This book is a work of fiction. Names, characters, businesses, organizations, places, events and incidents either are the product of the author's imagination or are used fictitiously. Any resemblance to actual persons, living or dead, events, or locales is entirely coincidental.

For information contact: lynxelizabeth1@gmail.com / http://www.elizabeth-lynx.com

Book and Cover design by Elizabeth Lynx

Photography by Feedough

Contents

Fake Marrying the Billionaire

Dear Mysterious Woman in Jail Cell Next To Mine,

You're the one. The woman I am meant to marry. The fact that I don't know what you look like or even your name, is no concern of mine. Well, maybe a little. But you sound hot.

Wait, that doesn't sound right, let me try again. I'm a billionaire. Even the huge gossip site, Masked Eyes, calls me *devilishly handsome* and *billionaire I'd like to bang.*

My publicist is telling me to erase the previous paragraph but I don't think I will because I want you to know that I got a lot going for me. Someone that many women would love to marry but I am choosing you.

Will you marry me? No pressure, but I need to know soon. I have an inheritance depending on it.

Yours Matrimonially,

Hamish Blackwell

Chapter One

HAMISH

The moment I removed my sunglasses and stepped into the Hard Grind coffee shop, I couldn't help but notice all eyes turned toward me. A few mouths fell open, but that was to be expected. I had been labeled as *devilishly handsome* and the *billionaire I'd like to bang* by the gossip site, Masked Eyes.

I nodded to a few people seated at a nearby table. I hadn't the faintest idea who they were, but they obviously knew me by how they lowered their voices and whispered, "Oh my god, it's him."

I had been dealing with fame and recognition since I was a little boy. It came with being one of the richest men in America—as in the country, not the county.

One woman pointed, so I politely waved. When I was young, my tutor taught me to appreciate the attention. That I should see it as something to humble me. Their praise was worth more than any dollar I had in the bank, and I had billions.

Did I mention I was a billionaire?

Born rich and with good looks, I had it all. But I refused to let it go to my head. Here I was, at a regular coffee shop, amongst the non-billionaires, grabbing a regular morning coffee. The elite would never come to an establishment like this. They would head over to the Blue Bean over at the exclusive resort down the street or, more likely, have their assistant grab their morning beverage for them.

But I thought of myself as a regular guy who just happened to possess money, and lots of it.

I frowned when the line of people waiting to order parted as I approached. That wasn't necessary. I'd happily wait like anyone else.

But if they insisted…

With a sigh, I placed my hand on the dark wooden counter. The woman with long chocolate curls that fanned over her shoulders blinked up at me.

She was clearly nervous, and really, who could blame her? I was positive she had never met someone as wealthy as me before. I sometimes wondered if people thought my abundance would rub off on them. It won't, but it was a nice fantasy.

"Can I… uh, help you?" Her eyes slid to the side, refusing to meet mine.

"I'll take a cup of your premium roast."

"Of course. Yes. I just have to head into the back to grab a bag. It may take a few minutes. Why don't you have a seat and wait?" She waved at the now-empty tables that dotted the shop floor.

That was odd. I turned my back for less than a minute, and the place emptied out. I shrugged. It must be that everyone needed to head to work.

"Don't I have to pay first?" I asked, fully aware of how transactions worked.

"What?" She appeared surprised by my question. Her fingers played with her lower lip. "Right. Uh, okay."

The woman was quite attractive now that I had a good look at her. Her cheeks were a healthy pink, and her hair was thick and lustrous.

I was considering asking her out after I have my coffee. I smirked as I thought about how she'd gloat to her friends that she got to date a billionaire.

My friend James Diaz, the Vidtuber, recommended this coffee shop to me, and now I knew why. Excellent service and a pretty lady behind the counter, with no formality to be seen. It was refreshing yet curious, like an Edward Hopper painting.

She tapped away at the register. Once she told me the price, I slipped her my card.

She held it up, examining it closely. "Hamish Blackwell," she muttered.

"Yes, in the flesh." I waved a hand at myself amusedly.

She swallowed, her hands shaking, but she went back to what she was doing.

"I never caught your name?"

She had no nametag, and I wanted to know her name before I asked her on a date.

"Uh, Susannah." She refused to look at me as she slid the card toward me on the counter, along with the receipt.

I picked up both, shoving them into the pocket of my wool slacks.

Perhaps I wouldn't ask her out. She was too nervous for my liking. As much as I appreciated a woman I could impress with a nice dinner or a ride in my custom-made Lamborghini Estoque, I wasn't about to go out with someone who wouldn't even look me in the eye.

"I'll be at the table by the window." I pointed over.

She nodded and then dashed into the back. The plastic drape flapped as she pushed through it.

I shook my head. The whole morning had been odd. My PR manager kept trying to call me, which was silly since she knew I never answered the phone before ten in the morning. My lawyer, Jenner, left a few messages too.

My grandfather had passed last week. His will was being read this morning. I skipped it, much to Jenner's chagrin, but I already knew what it had to say.

I would receive the bulk of my grandfather's money. His homes, the various businesses he owned, and definitely the Castle Ridge land. That was the most important part to me. He knew it, and so did I.

My father died when I was five, and my mother, well... I hadn't seen her in years. Last I heard, she was finding herself somewhere in the Western Ghats mountain range.

The only other family member who had a chance of inheriting anything from my grandfather was my weasel cousin, Dickinson Isaac Conan Kerry. Since his first name matched his acronym, I always called him Dick. He hated that because deep down, he knew he would always be a tiny, shriveled dick.

My grandfather hated him too, but he knew the importance of family. I was sure Dick would inherit something. Perhaps our great-great-great-grandmother's set of golden phalluses she acquired from Queen Victoria. They'd be perfect for Dick.

I settled into the small wooden chair that gave a view of the main street of this tiny mountain town of Castle Ridge. My grandfather owned most of the land. The shop owner probably had no idea I now owned the land her shop was on. Susannah might be the owner, but I wasn't sure. Maybe she was just an employee.

Wait. James told me he was dating the owner, but he said she had red hair. I glanced back toward the counter. The woman was still in the back.

I guessed Susannah wasn't the owner.

My phone buzzed in my back pocket. I groaned and took it out. It was a text from Jenner. It was just past ten in the morning, so I could respond now.

Was it wrong to want mornings free of stress? No. I was a billionaire, and I deserved a perk like that.

When I swiped the phone to life, the text popped up as urgent. I rolled my eyes. Jenner thought everything he had to tell me was urgent.

Tapping it open, I noticed he had texted me ten times this morning. "Jesus," I muttered.

Scrolling to the top of the texts, I read them. My eyes widened as I realized why my lawyer was urgently trying to reach me before ten in the morning.

"That fucking weasel."

I quickly tapped the phone icon and called Jenner. It didn't take long for him to answer.

"You got my messages, Hamish?"

"Yes."

"Good. I lost my phone a few days ago and had to get a new one. I was worried my texts weren't getting through."

I shook my head. "Are you sure that's right, Jenner? Not about the phone, but about the will. Grandfather was old-fashioned and sexist and, if I'm being honest, a racist, but he would never expect me to do that for his inheritance."

It was antiquated and completely ridiculous.

"Those are the terms. And it's your grandfather. You know the will is iron-clad. There's no lawyer you could get on Earth, me included, who has any hope of challenging it. This will, Hamish, was written a decade ago and hasn't been updated since."

I frowned. "But his mental state wasn't really sound over the past few years."

"Like I said, it was drawn up ten years ago. He was completely in his right mind then. Once your mother ran off to the other side of the world, the only family members left whom he accepted were you and your cousin Dickinson."

"There must be a law against this? It's the twenty-first century. There's no way I'm doing that."

I had my pride.

"Then Dickinson gets everything, and you get nothing," Jenner said without an ounce of emotion.

"I have money. My *own* money. My *own* businesses. I'd still be a billionaire," I said as my nose flared.

I watched as people strolled past, dried leaves crunching under their feet. Those lucky jerks didn't know how good they had it. They weren't being threatened by a dead man to marry against their will.

"Barely. I hate to say it, Hamish, but your businesses aren't making the money they once did. And the Brazilian government seized your rainforest hotel last month after the Rainforest Rights Activists kidnapped your guests."

I groaned and rubbed my forehead. "I admit, that hotel was a mistake. I was kind of drunk when I came up with the idea. And being a few years ago I believed all my ideas were perfect. I had a bit of an ego back then."

"You still do," Jenner mumbled.

My brows pinched. "What did you say?"

"Nothing. The point is, your thirtieth birthday is in three weeks. That is your deadline. Get married by then or lose everything."

"And if I don't, Dick gets it."

That was madness. Dick was a millionaire and was always jealous of my billions. He hated that Grandfather loved me and only tolerated him. If he got the inheritance, he'd never let me live it down.

"Yes, and Hamish?"

"Yes?"

"Dick would then be richer than you."

No. I shook my head. That toad licker couldn't be the one with all the money. I wouldn't allow it. It wasn't so much my ego that would take a hit—even though it would very much take a hit from him having more money. Dick was the type of guy who loved money and power. He loved to hurt people. He would own this beautiful little town and tear it apart, piece by piece, until it was nothing but a giant crater where a mountain once stood.

Thankfully, my grandfather never brought him to his estate here. Shit, Dick would inherit that too.

Susannah wouldn't have the coffee shop to go to every day for work. Those people walking by on the sidewalk?

There wouldn't be any sidewalk to crunch leaves on anymore. I'd seen what Dick did once he got his hand on any property in the past. He either turned things into shopping malls or parking lots. That was what Castle Ridge, Virginia, would turn into. One giant mall with a huge parking lot.

Easy money in his eyes, with little maintenance.

He hated people and loved to ruin lives. He was greedy, vindictive, and got his kicks bullying whoever stood in his path.

Did I want my grandfather's money? Of course, I did; I was human, after all. We all wanted more than we needed. But what was more important to me was making sure Dick didn't get anything.

"And if I do marry, he gets nothing. Not even my grandfather's special penny collection."

My grandfather, in his last years, started to collect pennies. Not old or collectible pennies, just pennies he found on the street. Like I said, he wasn't all together there at the end.

"Not even the pennies."

"What about Dick? Is there anything that could disqualify him from inheriting the money?"

My cousin was no saint. Perhaps there was something in his past that would make it impossible for him to get the money.

"Only if he committed tax fraud. Then it would automatically go back to you, whether you were married or not."

"What? What about murder or rape or any number of horrific things that I am blanking on right now?"

"Nope."

"He's probably committed tax fraud. It's Dick. So, no marriage." Hope rose in my chest.

"You would think, but I met his latest tax attorney at a party two months ago. Apparently, his old one died. Anyway, he told me Dick wanted everything by the book. And his new attorney was your grandfather's old attorney, so he's a good one."

Damn it.

I took a deep breath and watched as an orange leaf floated to the ground right outside the window. These people deserved better than what my cousin would offer them.

"Do I have to stay married to her?"

"For at least two months. That's the timeframe in the will."

I nodded, even if Jenner couldn't see me. It wasn't forever. By early January, I could start the divorce proceedings and be a free man once again by spring. Maybe even sooner if we got the right judge.

This wasn't my life, just a few months. No big deal. I forced a smile, and I swallowed the bullshit I was telling myself.

"Okay. I'll get married before my thirtieth birthday."

Why did it feel like I was losing a limb?

"There's one very important detail about who you should marry that's in the will."

"Oh, for fuck's sake. Is it bad? He's not making me marry one of my exes, is he?" Because the women I dated in the past were more like Dick in their lust for money. I was blinded by their beauty and charm. Okay, maybe it was their tits… but I was young.

Since I turned twenty-five, I vowed never to be in a relationship with a woman again. I slept with them, went out on dates occasionally, but never anything long-term.

"No, not one of your exes. But he does require that your new wife be a, uh…"

"Just spit it out."

"A virgin. She must be a virgin on your wedding night. And twenty-one years of age."

My palms began to sweat, and I nearly dropped the phone. "A twenty-one-year-old virgin? I've never dated a twenty-one-year-old virgin in my life, even when I was twenty-one."

I had a thing for older women. They knew what they were doing in bed. I enjoyed being with someone who knew how to pleasure me and reveled in the pleasure I gave back.

Right as I was about to refuse Jenner and accept that my asshole cousin would own this town, the door to Hard Grind opened with a bang.

I glanced up in surprise as several police officers ran into the shop with guns raised and surrounded me. I heard Jenner calling out as I dropped my phone.

"Stand up very slowly, Hamish Blackwell, and put your hands behind your back," one of the cops said.

"What the hell? I think you have the wrong Hamish Blackwell." I stood and put my hands in the air.

One of the cops tilted his head toward a corkboard that held an array of fliers. "You look an awful lot like the Hamish Blackwell on the wanted poster right there."

I narrowed my eyes as I scrutinized the photo in the flier. I gasped when I realized it was my business photo—the same one used on my biography on several of my corporate sites. There I was in a suit, smiling for the camera.

"What the hell am I wanted for?" My brain raced to figure out what would cause my arrest.

Was this about the hotel in Brazil? I let the Brazilian government take control of that a month ago when all the kidnapping happened.

"You're wanted in the death of Tiberius Endicott."

I felt the blood drain from my face as an officer forced me to turn and slapped cuffs on my wrists.

I was wanted for murder?

Chapter Two

JAMI

"What's his name?" the officer asked, petting my rooster.

I pushed my glasses up the bridge of my nose. "Nancy."

Thinking about Nancy and Nathan made my heart pump faster in my chest. I twirled some strands of my blond hair around my finger, then I released the hair before grabbing another lock and starting over again. The repetition helped me not collapse into a puddle on the jail cell floor.

After what I did, I wondered if I'd ever be let out. Julia wasn't going to be happy, and I couldn't blame her. I thought I could care for her son, but I was wrong. And now I was paying the price.

"That's a girl's name," the officer who arrested me said as his brows pinched.

People did that when they were confused, which happened a lot around me. My sisters and parents were the ones who rarely did that with me. They loved me as I loved them. But now they might pinch their brows at me too, disappointment replacing the love in their hearts.

My ears burned. I needed Nancy.

"It's his name. He helps me." I stared at the wall, unable to watch him with Nancy. I knew Nancy didn't like to be held like that. It pained me to watch him hold my rooster and crush him like that.

"You a farmer?" he asked.

I shook my head. "Where's Nathan?"

"Don't worry, Ms. Nutters. Your son is being looked after by Officer Henry."

"He's not my son. He's my nephew."

He was about to say something when there was some commotion coming from down the hallway.

Castle Ridge wasn't a big town, and the police station's size reflected that. There were only two cells. The arresting officer told me the one I was being held in was reserved for females.

The other, which was immediately to my right, separated by a cement wall, was reserved for men. While I couldn't see if anyone was in the men's cell, I suspected it was empty since there was no noise coming from it.

I had only ever seen jail cells on the true crime shows I watched with Laura. She was always so amazed at how I figure out the criminal so quickly.

It was just like figuring out a puzzle. I just needed to put all the right pieces together.

I lowered my head into my hands. How had I screwed up so badly? I had read the manual thoroughly before I took off in my sister's car. There should have been no reason for the car to break down.

While I didn't want to break the law, I knew it was a necessary evil so my nephew could get to the doctor.

The noise grew louder, and I heard a man shouting. I heard something about how the police were making a mistake and that he owned the town.

There was a bang, and I lifted my head. The sound of metal scraping metal. There was an officer—a different officer—off to the right speaking to someone in the men's cell.

"Okay, big guy. You got your phone call, and now you wait. If your friend can bail you out, you can go, but know the judge set the bail at a million dollars, so I doubt—"

"I'm a fucking *billionaire*. That's nothing to me." His voice was deep, and for some reason, it made me shiver.

Even weirder, heat bloomed between my legs, and my cheeks warmed. Thoughts of when my sister, Julia, explained fuck-me voices to me filled my head. He had one.

She was always comparing men about sex. How good they would be at it or if they were hot enough.

"Well, Daddy Warbucks, quit your complaining because you'll be home soon enough." I recognized the cop as he sneered at the guy in the cell. It was Officer Johnson. He had been on the force for ten years and was about my oldest sister Julia's age, which was thirty.

Once Officer Johnson saw me, he smiled. "Hey, Jami, what are you doing here?"

I began twisting my hair around my finger again. "I don't have a license."

"Okay. But why would you be in the holding cell for not having a license?"

My eyes fell to his feet. His shoes were black and scuffed up, and there was a permanent wrinkle that arched his toe line.

"I was driving Laura's car."

"Oh, well, you shouldn't drive without a license, but I don't think that means you get thrown in jail. Let me talk to Sheriff Lana, I'm sure—"

"The car. It caught fire. And then Officer Kolsti wanted to take Nancy from me, but I wouldn't let him. And when he tried to take Nathan, I yelled… at him."

I was embarrassed. I hadn't lost my temper in a long time. Over the years, I had worked hard to accept what I could not control. Nancy helped with that.

And Nathan… well, he made me realize that love and acceptance were more important than any irritation, like a change in plans or a different routine.

"Look, I'm sorry," he said, and I glanced up into his blue eyes. "Officer Kolsti is new. He's not used to how things are done around here, ya know?"

I shrugged. I didn't understand, but I learned over the years that it was best to shrug when it seemed everyone else knew what was going on, even if I didn't.

"I'll call your sister and make sure Nathan is okay."

I nodded.

"And, hey," he said with a whispered tone.

I glanced over at him, and he waved me over. I stood from the blue plastic bench and walked up to the metal bars that separated us.

"I'll get Nancy for you. There's no reason you can't keep him in here with you until Julia arrives."

"Yes." I nodded, but then scrunched up my face. "I mean, thank you."

Officer Johnson stared at me for a moment, and with a wink, he walked away.

I never understood winks. Laura, my middle sister, always told me they meant a secret. But then Julia told me it was men being sexy. When I asked if women were allowed to wink, she said yes. So was Officer Johnson telling me a secret, or was he just being sexy?

I sighed. At least I'd get Nancy back.

"He sure does like you. I wish I had a friend on the force," the guy in the cell next to mine said.

"He's not my friend."

"Oh, yes, he is. And based on what I heard, he wants to be more than a friend, if you know what I mean. He's letting you keep your friend Nancy with you."

I shook my head. "No, Nancy is a rooster."

There was silence for a few moments.

"A rooster? Are you a farmer?"

"No, I'm not a farmer."

"So, she's a pet?"

"Nancy is a male. Roosters are males—"

"Look, I'm not judging. I'm the last person to judge you or anyone when it comes to what type of pet you have, or if you have some friends on the inside, or dating or sex. I meant no offense."

"I'm not dating him, and I've never had sex with a guy."

My sister always got upset when I told people everything about that part of my life, but I never saw the problem with it. They called it too much information, but I just called it being honest.

I believed a lot of problems would be solved if people were honest with each other and stopped pretending or lying to one another.

"Oh, so you're a lesbian?"

I tilted my head. "Why would you think that?"

"You just said you never had sex with… Wait, are you a virgin?"

"Yes. Are you?"

There was silence.

It was surprisingly nice to talk to someone without seeing them. Refreshing even. I didn't have to worry if I should smile or frown. It wasn't always easy to figure out when someone was joking or being serious.

I found it best to assume they are being serious. That way they wouldn't take offense.

"How old are you?"

I noticed he didn't answer my question.

"I turned twenty-one on June eighth this past year."

"Holy shit. You're a twenty-one-year-old virgin. This must be a sign."

"What?"

"I meant that… You know what? It doesn't matter. How about we get to know each other? I'm—"

"Okay, you're free to go. Your sister's in Sheriff Lana's office. And here's Nancy," Officer Johnson said as he pulled open the cell door and held out my rooster.

I gasped, my heart racing as I set eyes on my wonderful rooster. I scooped up Nancy, and he instantly nuzzled his beak into my armpit.

Most of the anxiety washed away the moment I held him. I knew it wasn't normal to have a pet rooster, but I loved that bird.

Officer Johnson directed me out, but as he did, the man in the cell next to mine yelled something. I couldn't hear what he said, but I assumed he was telling me goodbye.

"Goodbye," I called back.

Once I was in Sheriff Lana's office, I saw Julia with Nathan in her arms. Relief consumed me, and I flopped into the chair next to Julia.

"Is he okay?" I asked, unable to take my eyes off my nephew.

"He's fine. Needs a change, though." Julia wrinkled her nose.

I set Nancy down and held out my arms. "I can do it."

"We don't have a changing room at the station, Jami," Sheriff Lana said.

I glanced around her office. She had a small couch against the wall, a metal filing cabinet against the other wall, and a round woven rug in the middle of the hardwood floor.

I pointed to the rug. "I can just do it right there. I tucked some emergency diapers and wipes in Nathan's carrier."

Both women glanced at each other. Julia turned back to face me, placing a hand on my arm.

My sister only ever touched my upper arm when she thought I didn't understand something. She was trying to be kind, but I hated when she did that. She was the one who defended me when I was younger, when others called me stupid or worse. And yet here she was, treating me as if I were still a child and not an adult.

"It's not appropriate to change a baby in the middle of the sheriff's floor. We can head across the street to the coffee shop. They have a changing station in there." My sister nodded at me.

I gazed at my nephew, who was only two months old. He had been in that diaper for a while. His fists were tight, and I could tell he was uncomfortable.

"I don't care if it's not appropriate. We are responsible for his wellbeing. It's the police station's problem if they think babies don't exist. I'm going to change my nephew, with or without your permission." I reached over and scooped Nathan from my sister.

My sister's mouth fell open in surprise by what I said, though I never understood why people adhered to ridiculous rules. Rules that caused more harm than good and made things difficult.

I grabbed the diaper and wipes from the carrier. I also grabbed his blanket and used it to cover the rug. It took me less than a minute to change him.

"Do you have a bag? Like a grocery bag or something I can put the used diaper in?" Thankfully, newborn diapers were small. No one would be the wiser of what was inside once I wrapped it up in the brown paper bag the sheriff gave me.

I handed Nathan back to my sister. "I have to go wash my hands and throw away the diaper. I'll be back."

I turned to the door but stopped as I heard the sheriff say, "Actually, Jami, I'll have Officer Kolsti throw the diaper out for you. Just place it on the corner of my desk before you leave."

My eyes widened. "But he didn't change Nathan, I did —"

"He needs to learn about the needs of the community. He needs to learn about the people of the community. What he did to you wasn't right. He should have helped you, not assumed the worst and had you arrested. It wasn't your fault the car caught on fire."

"I thought it just broke down. Laura's not going to like that her car burned up," Julia said.

"I've had a talk with him, but I think the diaper removal will help drive home the importance of helping people instead of what he did."

"He's not going to like that," I pointed out.

There were a lot of people in this town who didn't like me. Their only reason was that I existed. That's what Julia told me when I was nine, when some kids locked me in a broom closet at school. I remember the closet and being worried my mom wouldn't know where I was, but it was Julia who told me the teachers had blamed me.

I loved Julia. When I was young, I thought she was like Wonder Woman, fighting for justice. But now that I was an adult, it felt as if she were trying to keep me a child.

"Oh, I know." The sheriff smiled.

The last thing I wanted was for more people in the town to hate me.

I looked down at the bag in my hands. "No, I don't want that."

"But, Jami, he was a jerk to you." Julia stood after placing Nathan back into his carrier.

"People have bad days. And he's new. Maybe he thought he was impressing you by bringing someone in," I said, even if I was only guessing.

"Jami, you don't understand—" Julia said as she lifted Nathan's carrier, but I held up my hand.

"No, Julia, *you* don't understand. I'm not a child. Yes, I have autism, but that doesn't make me an idiot."

"No, honey, I wouldn't think that for one moment. I'm sorry if I made you feel that way."

I gazed at her, trying my best to understand how she felt, but I couldn't. I saw the same expression she had given me all her life—the one that said she knew what was best for me, and I didn't.

"Then why do you treat me like one?"

Chapter Three

HAMISH

Every person in the station glared at me and acted as if I murdered kittens as a hobby. One officer pointed at his eyes and then pointed at me—the universal symbol of letting me know he was watching me.

"Man, they despise you." Jenner's brown eyes crinkled in amusement.

I stared at his thick auburn hair as he ran his fingers through it. The man was vainer than anyone I knew. I bet he was getting himself ready in case there were photographers out front of the station.

"Obviously. They think I killed someone."

"Tiberius Endicott." Jenner checked his phone before slipping it back into his navy suit pocket.

"I don't even know anyone by that name," I mumbled as I glanced over my shoulder at the crowd of hate forming behind me.

We stood at the front desk of the station. Jenner was signing documents, and I was handed a large envelope with my things.

I checked my wallet because I wouldn't put it past these bumbling cops to nick a few bills from me.

"Is it all there?" Jenner glanced up from the desk, his fingers gripping a pen.

"Yes." I glared back at the cops, letting them know how it felt to have the cold eyes of suspicion thrown at them.

Jenner stood and waved me toward the door. Once I stepped outside, flashes went off, blinding me.

He guided me toward a limo, and I climbed inside.

"Way to go incognito." I pointed at the interior of the vehicle as Jenner slid in beside me and closed the door.

"I came directly from dealing with a politician in DC. They always drive around in town cars and limos. It's what I had on hand." He shrugged and pulled out his phone. "Now, where are we going?"

"Head to The Blue Spot. I'll talk to Rock. He might be able to help."

Rock Diaz was the owner of an exclusive resort in Castle Ridge, Virginia. It opened earlier this year and was a huge success. It was an old estate from one of the oil barons of the nineteenth century, and only the elite stayed there. Rock bought the property, modernized it, and named it The Blue Spot.

I had met his brother Monty at university. He went to MIT, and I went to Harvard. We were right down the street from one another. Once I met his brother Rock, we hit it off. And their younger brother, James, was fun, too—a little immature, but a nice guy.

The resort was about twenty minutes away on the outskirts of town, overlooking the Blue Ridge Mountains. The area was beautiful and peaceful. And since it was

October, the changing leaves made everything burst with color.

As I stepped out of the limo, I understood why Rock wanted to open the place. Imagine living with mountains and trees and wildlife all year round. No more chaos from the city.

I took a deep breath. It even smelled like heaven.

Rock stepped out of the resort and waved at me.

"Did you tell him we were coming?" I asked Jenner.

"Yes. Your face and name are everywhere with this murder. I needed Rock to find a location where you can hide for a while." Jenner guided me toward the entrance.

"Hide?" I waved my arms around. "But we're in the middle of nowhere."

"There are still people in this town and at the resort. They can't know you're here, or the paparazzi will descend on you."

I gazed around and saw a few people walking toward their cars. One man stared at me, and after a few seconds, he lifted his phone like he was filming me.

Shit. Jenner was right. I lifted the collar of my wool coat to hide my face.

Once we were inside, Rock ushered us toward a small hallway. I gazed around and didn't recognize this part of the building.

The main part of the building was made of dark wood-paneled walls with large oil paintings. And the lobby had a mosaic tile design on the floor that was breathtaking. But the hallway we were currently walking down seemed old. The walls were plain white, and an old, thin green carpet covered the floor.

"Where are we?" I asked.

"The old servants' quarters. In between the walls, so to speak," Rock said as he glanced over his shoulder at me. "It hasn't been updated yet. The carpeting was put in during the forties. Where we're going is a separate part of the resort, only connected by a hallway."

That was both fascinating and disgusting all at once.

"I'm taking you to stay in one of the servants' wings."

"But aren't people already staying there?"

We made our way to a dark brown door with a worn brass knob. Jenner and I had to step back so Rock could open it. Once he had it opened, we stepped through.

It was another hallway, but wider. The walls were lined with doors similar to the one we just walked through.

"No. Like I said, this part hasn't been updated, so it's not up to code."

I frowned. "You're making me stay here?" I took a step toward one of the closed doors and opened it.

There was a sound coming from inside, and I jumped back. A figure scurried across the floor.

"What was that?"

"Probably a squirrel. One of the old vents isn't secured properly, so some animals get in here. I suggest you pick one of the rooms on this side of the hallway." Rock pointed to the door near him.

I swiveled toward him, my eyes wide. "But this is an exclusive resort... and you have animals running through here."

"That's why this area is closed off until it's fixed. We've updated about ninety-five percent of the property. Since we didn't need this area back in June when it opened, we put off the renovation. But there's one small thing you should know that you probably won't like."

A shocked laugh burst from my throat. I threw my hands up in the air. "What could be worse than having to live in a squirrel-infested room?"

Rock scratched the back of his head. "The contractors will be here on Monday. So, the good news is the animal problem will soon be gone. The bad news is you have to hide in the attic when they arrive."

I rubbed my face. This day had gone from bad to worse. "Look, I appreciate what both of you have done for me, but I'm not staying here. I'll find a rental. There must be rental properties in the area."

I gazed over at Jenner, who was holding his phone high toward the ceiling. "There's no reception back here."

"Not likely. This place is really sealed off. You could scream your head off back here, and no one would hear you," Rock said with a chuckle.

His laughter quickly died once he saw my face.

"I'm not staying here, Jenner. Find me some other place to live."

"That may take a few days. You can live here right away."

"What about the room I was staying in? You know, the one on the third floor that overlooked the mountain? Why can't I keep staying there?"

Jenner and Rock gave each other a look. Rock sighed and stepped toward me. "You're my friend, but I've been listening to what the guests and even the staff have been saying. As messed up as it sounds, I think it's more that you are a billionaire that's angering them."

"They're pissed because I have money?"

"No." Jenner slipped his phone into his jacket pocket. "They think you are a billionaire who murdered someone, and now you're walking free *because* of your money."

My eyes bounced between the two men as I digested Jenner's words. I didn't think Jenner was right. But despite that, I had to figure out why I was a suspect for Tiberius Endicott's murder—whoever that was.

I couldn't do that while the paparazzi were hounding me.

"Okay. I'll stay here for as long as it takes you to find me a rental. Even a place to buy. *Something.*"

Jenner leaned close to me and lowered his voice. "I'll get working on that. Now, I hate to change the subject to something just as bad, but have you given any thought about the marriage idea we discussed earlier today?"

"Marriage?" Rock's face widened in surprise. "Are you going to get married?"

I smiled. "Yes."

"What?" Jenner and Rock blurted out at the same time.

"I think I found the perfect woman who will fit my grandfather's requirements."

"Grandfather's requirements? Didn't he die?" Rock asked.

"Yes. It's part of his will. If I don't marry a twenty-one-year-old virgin by my thirtieth birthday, I'll lose out on his inheritance."

Rock shook his head. "So? You have money."

"Then it goes to Dick."

Rock's confused expression slowly fell into horror. "Oh, god, no. You can't let that happen, Hamish."

"I know." I leaned my hand against the wall but quickly pulled it away when I realized the wall was sticky. I swallowed back the bile that rose in my throat and wiped my hand on my pants. "That's why I said I was getting married. And the woman. Perfect. She admitted she was twenty-one and a virgin."

Jenner held up his hands. "Of course she admitted that to you. You're Hamish Blackwell. She knew you were a billionaire and told you what you wanted to hear."

I shook my head and pushed my finger into his shoulder. "She never saw me. She doesn't know what I look like or my name."

"But how?" Rock asked.

"She was in the cell next to me. I never saw her, and she never saw me."

There was silence.

"You met this woman in… in jail?" Jenner asked.

I nodded. "Perfect, right?"

But then my words clicked together in my brain like a squirrel jumping on me at night in bed.

"Shit. I never got her name."

Both men let out a breath, almost like they were relieved.

"I'm sure we'll find someone else, Hamish." My lawyer came over and placed an arm over my shoulder. "Someone without a criminal record. Okay?"

"Maybe," I said with a sigh.

I was tired and hungry, and the last thing I wanted to do was sleep in any bed in this part of The Blue Spot.

"How's Monty doing?" I asked to distract myself.

Rock shook his head. "He came back to win over Julia and instead made things worse. You know... the usual."

"I think I mentioned a dinner party to him. Maybe you could get Laura to convince Julia to throw a dinner party tonight. Secretly invite Monty, and me too, of course," I said with a smirk.

I originally thought up the idea of the dinner party to get a chance to meet the third Nutters sister. Now I just wanted an excuse to eat and do it somewhere other than here.

Rock rubbed his chin. "You know, that's not a bad idea."

Of course it wasn't. I never came up with bad ideas, except maybe the rainforest hotel in Brazil. I was humble enough to admit I made mistakes.

Rock's girlfriend, Laura Nutter, was a chef. The dinner party would be wonderful, and that wasn't just my stomach talking.

Chapter Four

JAMI

They were whispering.

I tried to ignore my sisters, but it was difficult. Even as I chopped the carrots for the salad, I heard their voices, like mice scurrying over floorboards.

My jaw tensed, but I focused on the knife in my hand. Cooking was one of the few things I enjoyed. I wasn't as talented as my sister Laura, who was a chef at The Blue Spot just outside of town. Her boyfriend, Rock, owned the resort.

But it was the prep work I enjoyed the most. The things a lot of people hated to do, I found pleasure in. The chopping and measuring helped me focus.

The whispers grew louder.

With a sigh, I put the knife down.

"I can hear you two." I pushed my glasses up the bridge of my nose and moved into the family room. Laura and Julia were both seated on the blue couch and turned to face me.

Their smiles, insincere at best, told me exactly what they were up to. It was the same grins that screamed "pity tinged with love."

I spent the last decade studying my family's expressions. I knew how they felt, even if they never told me.

"Laura was just asking about her car." Julia waved at our sister.

"I'm sorry. It stopped for no reason. I didn't realize it was on fire until the cop tapped on my window." I walked around the couch and sat on the leather wingback chair by the front window.

"How did you not know?" Laura asked.

I blinked. "I was focused on getting the car to start."

Laura frowned. And then she did something that caused me to sweat. She rubbed her brow. My sister only did that when she was frustrated—and that emotion rarely entered her life.

She was my relaxed sister, the one who never caused a problem. I wished I were more like her, always knowing just what to do. Laura would have handled the situation with the officer better. She never would have been arrested.

"I'm not angry, Jami."

Uh oh. She was annoyed. I hated when people said one thing, but their expression told me something else entirely.

"It's just… you took my car without my permission, and then you didn't even notice when it caught fire."

My eyes shifted to the ground, and I remembered I left Nancy in the backyard for some fresh air. I could really use my rooster right about now.

"I am sorry." My mind raced with how I could fix the situation. "I can help fix the car."

"You don't know how to fix cars. You studied anthropology at university. Did you take a car mechanics course we don't know about?" Julia asked.

I shook my head. "No. But I can learn. The library should have books—"

"I'm not mad about the car, Jami," Laura said for the second time.

I tilted my head and lifted my eyes to her. "But you look mad."

Laura let out a breath and sat back into the couch cushions. "It's not about the car. What if that officer hadn't shown up? I agree, he should have never arrested you, but I am thankful he came along. The car was on fire, and you couldn't smell it."

"I smelled the smoke."

There was silence as my sisters stared at me. I thought for a moment they were satisfied. They wanted to know if I could smell the smoke, and I had.

It was Julia who frowned first. Why weren't they happy? I just wanted this to go away and my sisters to be happy again. I twisted a few tendrils around my finger that had brushed my cheek.

"You smelled it once the officer showed up?" Laura asked.

"No, before then."

Laura narrowed her green eyes. "How long before then?"

"Several minutes. Uh, three minutes, I think. Because I pulled over, and it was ten fifty-two and then—"

"Okay." Julia waved her hands in the air. "I get it. You smelled smoke with my baby in the car, and you didn't think it was dangerous? That you needed to get him out?"

My heart thundered in my chest. They were right. Why hadn't I removed Nathan right away? I knew that was the right thing to do in the situation—I had learned it many times. "If you smell smoke, then get out," my mother always told me. She was referring to the house, but it applied to cars too.

But for some reason, I didn't do that.

"I just wanted to start the car."

I thought if the car would start, then everything would be okay. But it didn't start, and everything wasn't okay.

Julia smiled at me, and it was filled with hurt. Bile crept up my throat. I should have thought of Nathan's safety. That was always the first thing on my mind when I was taking care of him, but I only thought of the car.

The stupid car.

Laura pushed down on her skirt, brushing out wrinkles that weren't there. She took out her phone but tilted it up so I couldn't see her tap at it.

"I put in a new password. Don't try to memorize it, Jami."

It wasn't like I memorized the code on purpose. If I saw what she typed, my brain could recall it after that.

I stared at the floor. "I won't."

She sighed and glanced at her screen for a minute before she stood. "I guess I needed a new car anyway."

Laura walked out of the room, and I heard her head upstairs.

Tears pricked the corners of my eyes. She wouldn't even look at me. My sister, who had always been the one who understood me, even when I didn't myself, couldn't be in the same room as me. I had never seen her like that.

How could I have screwed up so badly? Maybe they were right… Everyone who ever told me I'd always need help. My teachers. The kids at school. Even the one guy I dated in college for a few months. He once told me I was a lot of work, among other terrible things, and I ended it with him the next day.

Maybe, just maybe, he was right. I couldn't be trusted to take a baby to his doctor appointment.

I had been so wrapped up in my own thoughts that I gasped when I felt Julia's hands cover mine. She had moved over to the matching chair next to mine, and I hadn't noticed.

"Jami, it's okay. We all make mistakes."

My cheeks burned, and I felt warm tears slip down my face.

"Not like this. I put Nathan at risk." The last word came out in a whisper. I couldn't speak anymore. If I did, it would turn into a sob.

"Laura just needs time to adjust that her car is gone. You know how she was with that thing. It was her baby. That car was going to die anyway. You just happened to be driving when it did."

My sister was lying to me. Flat-out lying. I blinked the tears away as I watched her. She never did that. She lied to others all the time, but never to me.

Or maybe she had, and I never realized it.

How many things had I been oblivious to in my life? My heart pounded. How many people had I hurt and never knew?

"Why are you saying this to me?"

She sighed and shook her head. "Because I love you. And I know you'd walk through burning coals to keep Nathan from being hurt. What happened today… it was just a mistake. Stress has a habit of causing us to make poor decisions." She raised her hand. "And I'm the queen of poor decisions."

"No, you aren't. It just takes you a while to trust people."

For a second, her face fell. What I said shocked her. She turned her head and cleared her throat. "Maybe." She turned back to face me. "Maybe, but I learned to trust you a long time ago."

I tried to pull my hands away, but she held on.

"And, Jami," she lowered her head to look in my eyes as I stared at the floor, "I still trust you. That will never change."

I loved my sister, and I knew she was just saying that to make me feel better, but what happened was dangerous. I needed to prove to both my sisters that I would never do anything to hurt them or the people I loved again.

"There's going to be a dinner party here tonight. I can make an excuse and tell people you're not feeling good if you want. I know you aren't big on crowds, so just take the night and rest in your room."

I sighed. That did sound good to me. When Julia had Nathan's one-month birthday a few weeks ago, she invited so many people. I hid in the kitchen with Nancy to keep watch over the food—not that it needed it—but at least food never expected conversation.

I was about to thank Julia when a thought entered my head. Something that could possibly make things better with Laura.

"No."

Julia's eyes widened. "What?"

I lifted my gaze and straightened my back. "No. I will be at the dinner tonight. In fact, I'll try that cranberry recipe I've always talked about."

Her brow wrinkled. "Grandma's recipe? Are you sure?"

"You don't think I can make it?"

She shook her head. "No, it's not that. The recipe is actually pretty simple."

I frowned.

"I mean, it's a great recipe to start cooking with, Jami. You are super helpful with prepping the food and making sure we have all the ingredients. Laura's always thankful for your help. You've always talked about cooking, but never actually did it. Why now?"

I forced a smile like my sisters had earlier. "To help make up for what happened to the car."

It was a lie. My palms were sweating, and I had a tremendous urge to scream, but I sat there, forcing that grin to stay in place.

"You really don't have to—"

"I want to."

Julia nodded. "Okay. Sounds great."

My sister got up and headed toward the stairs. I blinked. It worked. The very first lie I had ever told in my life worked.

Maybe there was something to it. Julia lied to me because she said she loved me, and to make me feel better. And she was right. When others told me the truth growing up, like the kids at school, it hurt.

The lie I just told was to help my sisters. I did it for love.

Chapter Five

HAMISH

"Wow, this place is small." I glanced around the entryway. "Is this the guest house? Perhaps I could sleep here instead of The Blue Spot... Ouch, that hurts."

I jerked my arm away from Rock as he pulled me into a slightly bigger room with a blue sofa.

"What is wrong with you?" Rock asked through gritted teeth.

"I should ask you the same question. We only just entered the Nutters' home, and you accost me. Dragging me into this quaint, uh... I want to say den, but I can see a dining table beyond the couch. Is this a trailer home? I've never been in one of those before."

Rock took a step back with confusion all over his face. "You think this stand-alone home is a trailer?" He shook his head. "You know, Monty mentioned you were a bit out of touch with the average person, but I had no idea you were this bad."

I arched my brow. "Come on, Rock. I'm the first to admit I was born with a silver spoon in my mouth."

"More like a diamond-encrusted spoon," he mumbled.

"Very funny. I admit, I don't know how the average person lives. That's a failing on my part. But how a person lives, or the home they live in, wouldn't prevent me from considering them an equal."

Rock's jaw tensed. "How very kind of you, Your Majesty."

"Rock, I can't help how I was raised. I had no control over my parents surrounding me with servants any more than you had control of where you grew up."

"Which was in a house about this size." He sighed and placed his hand on my shoulder. "I'm sorry. Perhaps I still get a little touchy about my past. And people who were raised in your world didn't treat my dad very kindly. It still gets to me sometimes."

I nodded. Rock was my friend. We met several years back, and I liked him the moment I met him. He was a hard worker and earnest. What he was saying about people with money was more common than I liked to admit.

I grew up with the top five percent. Most of them believed they were above the law and above the other ninety-five percent.

A thought popped into my head. *Above the law.* Glancing around the small room, I realized I was the one viewed as getting away with murder.

No wonder Jenner wanted me hidden. To the people of Castle Ridge, I was just another rich guy who could break the law and never pay for it. That was why Jenner said people didn't like me because of my money.

"I get it. I'm the bad guy." I rubbed my brow.

"No, you're not. I don't believe you killed anyone, Hamish. Whoever did this is framing you. I've met a lot of assholes who grew up wealthy like you, born with diamond-encrusted spoons in their mouths." Rock smirked. "Owning an exclusive resort like The Blue Spot means I run into a lot of them on a daily basis. But you aren't an asshole. Sure, you're conceited and oblivious to the hardships of the world, but in your heart, you are true."

I pointed out the window. "But what about them? To them, I'm already guilty. Whoever did this knew it would ruin me. No more most-eligible bachelor. Now I'm just the most-hated."

"Look, we'll have a nice dinner tonight and forget our troubles. Then, first thing tomorrow, I'll reach out to a few contacts I have and see what I can do."

I nodded. Rock was a good guy, a friend. The shock of the day was wearing off, and it was sinking in.

I was charged with murder.

Not only that, but in order for my weasel cousin to not get my grandfather's fortune, I had to marry a virgin. Even if one walked through the door, and I wined and dined her all night, what woman would agree to marry a potential murderer?

She'd have to be crazy or desperate. I swallowed. *Or both.*

I was so fucked.

A French door behind the dining table opened, and a group of women entered the room. They were beautiful and looked similar.

These must be the Nutters sisters.

I recognized Julia. She was the one who first informed me that not everyone liked me. I thought she was amusing and possibly flirting with me, but now, I realize she was right.

One of the women waved at Rock. That must have been Laura, his girlfriend. My eyes shifted to the other woman, the youngest.

She was the prettiest of them all, in my opinion. Maybe because her eyes were darker. I couldn't tell from here if they were brown or hazel, but there was something mysterious about them.

She glanced over at me, locking eyes. Normally when a beautiful woman caught my eye, I winked or smirked or did something to let her know I was interested, but I couldn't. Not with her.

It was strange. Something about her made me nervous. I hadn't been anxious like that since I was in tenth grade and asked out Summer Clyde.

The woman with her hair back in a ponytail moved forward toward us. "Rock, I thought you were coming later?"

"I wanted to bring my friend Hamish by before I went back out to, uh… grab the cookies, Laura."

They hugged, but as Rock mentioned the cookies, Laura stiffened and pulled back.

She narrowed her eyes at him. "I don't think the dinner party needs cookies."

"If Rock wants to bring cookies, Laura, then let him bring cookies," Julia said before snorting.

Laura turned to Julia and shook her head. "You don't understand, Julia. These cookies, they're uh… unwelcome.

The cookies need some time, maybe a little bit of distance. Then maybe they can be brought into this family."

I didn't think I was the only one who realized they weren't talking about cookies. Julia looked confused, as did the other woman.

"This is obviously a private conversation. I'm going to take Jami into the kitchen to help her with the cranberries." Julia's green eyes shifted to me. "Hamish, why don't you come help us?"

"Of course." I nodded and followed Julia and Jami around the blue couch toward the dining table. When we turned the corner, I was surprised to discover a kitchen.

It seemed the dining table was a part of the kitchen. While small, the kitchen was well-designed with white marble countertops, white cabinets, and a dark blue island with a wooden countertop. Despite the lack of room in the home, everything was nicely appointed.

"I'll warn you, I don't know the first thing about cooking," I said.

"That's okay. I just wanted to leave those two alone to let them work out their 'cookie' issue." Julia shook her head.

I glanced over at Jami. She had her arms wrapped around herself and appeared uncomfortable.

How rude. I hadn't introduced myself yet. No wonder she felt uncertain; she had no idea who I was.

"Hello. I'm Hamish Blackwell. Thank you for letting me be inside your charming home. It's lovely to meet you." I took a step forward and reached out my hand.

She stared at it for a few seconds and took a deep breath. Slowly, her arm moved. I would say she was hesitant to shake my hand, but it was something more than that. It was as if moving her arm physically hurt her.

Jami winced, her chin stiffened, and she stared at her hand as much as I did. Everything about her was rigid.

Even Julia gaped at her hand.

I couldn't take it anymore. The woman was obviously in pain. Reaching forward, I grabbed Jami's hand to shake.

And as stiff as she appeared, the moment I touched her hand, it felt like I had grabbed a handful of spaghetti.

I frowned. She frowned. Julia gasped in horror.

"I never knew your name," she said as she lifted her hand to shake.

Her hand almost slipped from mine, but I grabbed it in time. I had been in shock from the unusual handshake. When she went to move her hand for the shake, I had forgotten what we were doing.

"Of course not." I retracted my arm as quickly as I could.

The woman was beautiful and mesmerizing, but strange. I had encountered limp-wristed handshakes before in my life, but Jami's went way beyond that.

"Jami, are you okay?" Julia wrapped her arm around her sister.

"That was hard, but I'm okay," Jami said.

"Why don't you go out back?" Julia glanced over at me for a second before turning her attention back to Jami. "Get some fresh air, okay?"

"I have to cook the cranberries."

"You have plenty of time to do that. Why don't you show Hamish our backyard, and I'll rinse the cranberries for you?"

Jami's eyes lifted as she stared past me. "If you think that's okay."

"I do."

Maybe Jami wasn't feeling well. That must have been why she was hesitant to touch me, though that didn't explain her unusual handshake.

"I'd love to see the backyard. I bet you have great views of the mountains here."

"We have views of the trees. We live on the side of Castle Mountain. Until the leaves fall from the trees in five weeks, we won't be able to see the other mountains," Jami said and then brushed past me toward the French doors.

She opened the door and left. I glanced over at Julia, who shrugged.

"You're just supposed to follow her. She's not the type of person to wait around for you."

"Right." I nodded and turned to follow Jami out the door.

It was starting to get dark out, and I felt a slight chill in the air. I looked around the small yard that had a few pieces of lawn furniture and a white ceramic birdbath.

Jami stood near the birdbath with her back to me.

"Hey," I called out as I made my way toward her. "Nice yard. You were right about the trees—"

She turned, and my eyes widened. She cradled a rooster in her arms.

No. It couldn't be.

My mind raced to the morning. The jail cell. Her name.

I pointed. "Is that… No, it couldn't be."

"Nancy. My rooster."

My mouth fell open. I had found her. The twenty-one-year-old virgin.

Chapter Six

JAMI

I knew it was him the moment I heard him speak.

"Jami, can you pass the potatoes?" Julia reached across the table.

I lifted the dark blue ceramic bowl and handed it to my sister. My attention was divided between the bowl and man with the deep voice seated next to Julia.

He was tall and dressed like Rock in a suit and tie. My father owned a suit that he wore once, and that was to Grandma's funeral.

The people I knew never wore them.

I guess where Rock's from men wear suits.

"Jami, I heard you made the cranberry sauce," Laura said.

"Yes."

The cranberry sauce. I had forgotten about that. Once I realized the guy from jail, Hamish, was in my home, Grandma's recipe didn't seem so important anymore.

I tried to concentrate while cooking the cranberries, but Hamish was in the kitchen the whole time. I felt his eyes on me, watching me.

It was strange, a sensation I had never felt before. Not bad, but different. My nipples hardened. I kept glancing back at him while he watched.

Julia kept trying to help. She tried to remind me I was cooking, but it didn't stop the heat of Hamish's stare from clinging to me.

Laura smiled. "I can't wait to try it."

I watched as Laura raised her fork with the vibrant red sauce dripping down. As much of a distraction as Hamish was, I still wanted the cranberry sauce to work.

I had decided on a two-step process. Impress Laura with my ability to be a quick learner; she was a chef, so food was most important to her.

If I made her a family recipe, showing her I could cook and that family was important to me, then she might not be mad at me anymore.

Even if she was still upset about the car after tasting the sauce, I wanted to speak to Rock. I needed to ask what I could do to prove to Laura I was a responsible adult.

"It smells wonderful." Julia smiled.

I glanced around the table. Everyone had taken a scoop of the sauce, everyone but me.

I don't like cranberries.

There was some noise after they slipped the cranberries into their mouths. But it was strange. No one was chewing. Perhaps I cooked the sauce too long. It turned straight to liquid.

"How is it?"

Monty puckered up his face and swallowed. He was Rock's brother and Julia's boss. Rock had gone to get him, which was also strange.

I thought he was getting cookies, but then he showed up with Monty. And Julia wasn't happy about that. I didn't think she liked Monty all that much right now.

"It's, uh… so *unique*," Monty said after a few breaths.

"Mmm, yes," Laura added. "Is that garlic I taste?"

I nodded. "That was an accident. I thought it was the dried ginger. But I notice you using garlic a lot, so I thought it would work."

"It certainly did something," Julia said.

Hamish glanced around the table and frowned. "No one's going to tell her?"

"Tell me what?"

Laura gasped, and everyone glared at Hamish.

"Hamish, don't you dare," Rock said.

I was confused as to what was going on. It seemed everyone knew but me, and I hated when that happened. It was frustrating. I just wished people would say what they meant.

"Come on." Hamish threw his arms in the air. "She's not a child."

I blinked. My ears burned. A memory flashed in my head. My father saying the same thing at this very dinner table when I was sixteen.

My mom begged my dad not to say anything, and he didn't. Instead, he got up and walked off. Decided to take a drive. He did that sometimes when he was upset.

I never did learn what my father wanted to say.

"No one here thinks that, Hamish. But she's our sister and—"

"And what, Julia?" I asked as I felt a tear prick the corner of my eye.

"Jami, I didn't mean anything. It's a nice dinner, and I just wanted things to remain in good spirits."

"Then why could I hear you and Monty yelling when he arrived earlier? It's okay for you two to not be in good spirits, but I can't? Whatever Hamish has to say, he can say it."

The room was so quiet, I could hear Nancy outside pecking at the siding of the house. I turned my attention to Hamish. He cleared his throat and sat up a little taller.

"Well? What were you about to say?" I asked.

"It was…"

He mumbled something, but I couldn't hear.

"What?"

He cleared his throat again. "Jami, the cranberry sauce was… well, disgusting. I normally love cranberry sauce, but I wouldn't take another bite of this if you paid me a billion dollars."

"I think she gets the point," Monty said with a grumble.

My nose flared, and I glanced around the table. Everyone was staring at their plate.

"Is that true? No one likes it?"

"I liked the color." Julia gave a half smile.

"But not the taste," I added.

My sister sucked in her lips and shook her head. "It was your very first time cooking, Jami. It just had a few spices it shouldn't have, like basil," Laura said.

"And I think I tasted cinnamon. Which you would think would work with this type of dish, but it really doesn't," Rock said.

My heart pounded faster and faster in my chest. It was good that they were criticizing me. I should want these tips so I didn't do it next time.

But the more they commented, the more it hurt.

"I was trying to be creative. The garlic was an accident, but the others… I thought it would work with the dish."

Laura waved her hand in the air. "It's fine, Jami. Learning to cook takes time. That's why you need to follow the recipe. At least until you are more comfortable with which flavors work together and which don't. It's best not to experiment with it until you've done it for a while."

But it wasn't fine. I saw the way everyone stared at me. I saw the pity in their eyes. It was the same way my family looked at me when they thought I couldn't handle something.

I clenched my jaw. I was sick of being treated like a child who didn't know any better.

"Also, tasting a recipe while you're making it helps, but I know you don't like cranberries, Jami," Laura said with a sad smile.

"I guess that's why I thought it was weird you wanted to make Grandma's cranberry recipe since you never liked it." Julia crinkled her brow.

Pushing the chair back, I stood from the oak wood table. "I have to go." I turned, making my way toward the stairs.

I heard them calling out my name, but I ignored them. Taking the stairs two at a time, I made it to my room and closed the door behind me quickly.

I felt lightheaded, and my hands shook. Tugging at the thin neckline of my yellow sweater, I let my skin breathe.

It was just a recipe. Why was I getting so upset that it didn't turn out right?

There was a knock on my bedroom door. Probably one of my sisters to remind me there are certain things I just can't do.

"Yes?"

"Hey, Jami… can I come in?"

It was Rock.

I took a deep breath and opened the door. I stepped back, waiting for him to enter.

He glanced around before stepping inside and closing the door behind him. Rock was a tall guy, and in my room, he appeared even bigger. He wore a suit, as usual, but his dark blue tie had been loosened.

"I'm sorry Hamish said that to you. He's my friend, and I invited him. He shouldn't have treated you like that."

That didn't make sense.

I tilted my head. "How did he treat me?"

"Telling you the cranberry sauce tasted bad."

"But it did."

He nodded and took a step closer, grabbing the white chair at my small one-drawer desk, taking a seat.

"Yes, but he didn't need to say anything. You had tried so hard—"

"Wait." I held up my hands. "He told me the truth, and you're apologizing for him? Did he send you up here to do that?"

"Unfortunately, no." Rock frowned.

"You wanted me to believe I had made a great cranberry sauce for what reason? What purpose would that serve?"

He waved his hand at me. "This. You getting upset and running off. Laura told me to be gentle with you. That you don't handle things well sometimes, and—"

"She *what*?" My nose flared, and my neck felt hot. I pulled at my sweater again.

"It's not that you can't do things. You obviously can. It's just that you need some help—"

I folded my arms and glared at Rock. "What? Like a child?"

"No, not like a child—"

"You're just like my sisters. I stupidly thought it was just them. That they still saw me as the little sister they had to protect. But you too? I'm twenty-one years old; I'm not a child. There are lots of things I can do."

I believed what they told me for so long. That there would be things I could never do. Had I messed up at times? Yes. Today especially, but I knew I could do better.

"I know you can."

"Do you know what it's like to go through life and have everyone you meet think you're less than? That you will never be able to accomplish much, always reliant on others?"

Rock's eyes fell and stared at the floor. The man was silent. Something crossed over his face, an expression I had never seen before.

"Yes." His voice was a whisper.

That surprised me. Rock was the most successful man I knew. He created and ran a luxury resort, yet he said he understood what I was going through.

"Then help me. No one tells me the truth. You saw it down there; only your friend Hamish was willing to tell me the food wasn't good. Probably because he didn't know me."

Rock chuckled. "No, that's just Hamish. It doesn't matter how well he knows you; he'd tell you the truth always, good or bad. It's actually the thing that brought us together."

"He seems like a nice guy. That's why I didn't mind talking to him today in jail."

Rock's face went from smiling to a frown. He stood and took a step toward me. "You met him in jail?" His gaze shifted around the room. "That's right. Laura told me some idiot cop, new to town, arrested you for the car fire, and Julia had to bail you out."

"While I realize the fire wasn't my fault, I take full responsibility for not getting Nathan out right away. That's why I need your help. I need to learn, to understand how to know what to do when something out of the ordinary happens. You must handle crises at your resort all the time, yet you know what to do. I have to prove to my sisters I'm a responsible adult, not someone they need to take care of forever."

Rock sat back down and rubbed his hands together. He started to mumble something under his breath.

After a minute, he stood and took a deep breath. "There's someone you can help."

"But it's me who needs the help."

"Jami, by you helping him, I think people will look at you much differently."

"Then who is it?"

If Rock knew someone who could train me to think on the fly, or even give the appearance that I knew what I was doing, that would be perfect. Then my sisters wouldn't treat me like a child.

"It's Hamish."

Chapter Seven

HAMISH

I couldn't believe I was standing in the house of the woman I met in jail earlier today. Even more unbelievable, she was gorgeous and sweet and kind.

There wasn't a thing I'd change about her, except maybe the cooking. That cranberry sauce was awful.

Other than that, she was perfect.

And now my best friend was telling me she needed help, and he suggested I was the one who could provide it for her.

Was there ever a better wingman than Rock? If there was, I never met him.

He waved me up the wooden stairs toward the back of the upper floor. The only hallway I noticed was narrow; all the walls were white, and the floor kept creaking.

Did people really live like that? I really had no idea. It all felt so cramped and plain to me.

Rock knocked on the simple white door, and it flew open with a gust. On the other side stood the woman I hoped to marry.

It wasn't possible. In the short time since I saw her downstairs, her beauty grew. Her braid, which was now slightly frayed, lay across her shoulder. No perfect styling, just natural allure. And the way her glasses framed her haunting brown eyes was adorable. Even her simple sweater that was worn and stretched out was charming on her slight frame.

I knew marrying her was not about love or even sex. In fact, it would be irresponsible of me to have sex with her. I had to keep the marriage all business.

But I felt more confident knowing it would be Jami at my side.

"Jami, I know you met Hamish in jail today."

"Yes."

I watched her full lips pucker as she gave her simple response.

"Do you know why he was put in jail?"

Shit. She didn't know the specifics. I thought Rock had told her. Would she be open to marrying me after she found out the reason I was in that cell?

I straightened my shoulders. If I wanted my grandfather's fortune, then I had to work for it. She would be my wife, after all. It was time for me to be a man and explain that I was wanted for murder.

"All I know is that he is a fucking billionaire."

My eyes widened; even Rock coughed in surprise.

Well, the girl has a mouth on her, that's for sure.

"I don't think I have ever heard you curse before, Jami."

Her eyes bounced between me and Rock. "But that's what he said. He told the officer at the station that he was a *fucking billionaire.*"

The memory flooded back. The cop made it seem like I would be there for a while because the bail was set for a million dollars. That was when I told him I was a fucking billionaire.

Rock turned to face me with a smirk. "I guess you are."

I rolled my eyes. "Yes, I'm a billionaire, but there's a problem. I'm also accused of murder."

Her eyes widened. "Who?"

"Some guy I never met."

"Then how could you have killed him?"

"Exactly." I waved my hand, proving my point.

Jami stepped forward until we were only inches from each other. "Then the police are wrong."

I breathed in her scent of cinnamon and lilacs. "Yes, they are."

She looked up at me and then at Rock before turning her attention back to me. "So, tell them."

"I did. But they don't like me since I'm a billionaire. They don't mind screwing with my life."

"That's not right. That's not right at all."

She kept talking but mumbled the last part. Something about people not liking her either. I must have misheard because who wouldn't like Jami?

"Look, Jami, that's where I think you two can help each other. You can work for Hamish. Help him figure out why they think he did it. Then everyone will know how hard you worked clearing a wrongly accused man, and you'll get paid."

"What?" both Jami and I said at the same time.

"No, Rock, I thought you brought me up here to get Jami to marry me."

Rock took a step back. "Hell no. I'm not going to let you marry my girlfriend's sister."

"But she's twenty-one and a virgin—"

Rock plugged up his ears and shook his head. "La, la, la… I can't hear you."

"I'm standing right here," Jami said.

"I know, but your sister would kill me if she thought I set up a marriage between you and Hamish."

"Why would that upset her? Laura's my sister; I have known her longer than you. Is something wrong with Hamish?"

I folded my arms, not happy my perfect wingman was turning into a perfect dud. "Yeah, Rock, what's wrong with me?"

Rock rubbed the back of his neck. "I like you, Hamish. You've been there for me more times than I can count. You're a good friend. But…"

"But what?" I took a step forward as Rock took a step back.

"You're not really known for being… faithful."

"I have never cheated on a girlfriend."

"Not so much that… You just aren't with them that long. Name one relationship that's lasted longer than a month in the past five years."

He thought he knew me so well. In his eyes, I was just a player out to dupe his girlfriend's sister. I couldn't believe he thought so little of me.

"How about Sara?"

Rock's eyes shot up. "The one you met in the Alps? You were only there for two weeks. I remember because I was with you at the time."

"Two weeks?" I shook my head. "I could have sworn that was two months."

"Nope, just two weeks. And by the end, you were complaining she was becoming clingy because she asked for your hotel room number."

That sounded bad, but there was more to it than that.

"It was other things too, not just the room number."

Rock folded his arms. "Like what?"

Lots of reasons for ending it with Sara popped into my head, but before I mentioned them, I realized how petty they seemed. Especially the one about how she didn't like fish. At the time, I thought it was narrowminded of her, but now I realized it was just her taste.

Had I been looking for an excuse to end it?

"That was the past. I'm not here to go through my dating past with a fine-toothed comb. This is just a business contract. A job. I would be hiring her to portray my wife, that's all."

"I don't think Jami is the person you need—"

"Why don't you let me decide?" Jami interrupted.

"Yeah, Rock, why don't you let her decide? She's a grown woman."

Jami gazed up at me, her eyes wide. There was something about that petite woman that made me want to pull her into my arms. She was innocence wrapped in strength.

After all that I told her about the murder charge and the marriage, she was standing here asking me questions. Lots of other women would have run out the door.

She studied me as if I said something profound. I swallowed the knot in my throat. Whatever she saw in me,

I most likely wasn't it. Yes, she was beautiful and sweet and checked off all the boxes for the wife I needed, but there would never be a long-term relationship. Just two months. I had to make it clear exactly what I wanted.

"Jami, I know it sounds strange, but in order for me to get my inheritance, I must marry a twenty-one-year-old virgin by my thirtieth birthday. And, in jail earlier today, you mentioned you were twenty-one and a virgin. I thought maybe you could help me out."

"That's extreme. Marriage. I see why you would pick me due to my age, but I never considered becoming someone's wife before."

I shook my head. "It's only for two months, so not long at all. And I can pay you."

Her brow wrinkled. I knew what she was thinking, and it wasn't good.

"No sex involved. I mean, not like a prostitute or anything like that. Ugh. This isn't coming out right." I rubbed the beads of sweat from my brow.

"But why me?"

"You're a twenty-one-year-old virgin. And I know your family—"

"No, you don't. You know the men dating my sisters. But this is the first time you've been in our home. And I didn't meet you until today."

She was right. I met a beautiful young woman in jail today, and I knew I had to marry her—not that I saw her beauty, but that didn't matter.

I had to convince her that *she* was the one.

My mind raced with any little details about Jami I could find.

"You're quirky."

"*Quirky*?" both Rock and Jami blurted out at the same time.

I shrugged. "Yeah, sort of. Uh, what about Nancy? You walk around with a rooster. Roosters are male, but yours has a female name."

"I like the name Nancy, so I named my rooster Nancy." Her eyes flickered toward the window. "That doesn't make me quirky. I'm not quirky or slow or stupid or—"

"Whoa!" I held up my hands. "That's not what I meant at all. I'm sorry if I made it seem like I was saying that, but I wasn't. I meant cute and fun."

I watched her for a moment as she turned to face the window, her back now to me. Her shoulders rose and fell rapidly. She was upset. I had touched a nerve.

"I think what Hamish was trying to say," Rock side-eyed me, "was that you're different from the women he usually dates."

Jami turned, narrowing her eyes at Rock. "But I'm not dating him."

"No, but marriage is, for some, the end goal of dating."

"Then why aren't you married to Laura? You've been dating my sister since the summer. It's now autumn."

Rock's eyes widened. I watched as my friend squirmed with an explanation to his girlfriend's sister's question. It was glorious.

"Yeah, Rock, put a ring on it, why don't you?" I said with a chuckle.

Rock rubbed the back of his neck and began to pace the small room, mumbling to himself.

Jami looked at me, and I her; neither of us had any idea what was going on.

"Rock, are you okay?" I reached out and put my hand on his shoulder, stopping him mid-stride.

"What? Yes, of course. I was just thinking that we really should go with my original idea of hiring Jami to help us *find* someone for you to marry. She knows the town and its people."

Maybe Rock was right. My focus shouldn't be on getting Jami to marry me at this exact moment. I was asking an almost stranger to marry me. What woman would say yes to that?

I took in Jami, really studied her. She stood there fidgeting with her fingers, her gaze shifting to the floor. It was obvious she was uncomfortable.

That was the problem. I had to make her comfortable. Let her get to know me. Then she'd see that the temporary marriage might be fun.

We could travel anywhere she wanted. I could buy her a new wardrobe or a car or anything she wanted. Once she saw the benefits of being my wife, I bet she'd be more open to the idea.

"I guess you're right, Rock. Jami, would you like to be my assistant while I'm here in Castle Ridge?"

"A job?" she mumbled.

"Yes, just a job. Complete with salary and benefits—"

"What sort of salary?"

The corner of my mouth curled. *Smart woman.* It was always wise to make sure you got what you were worth, not just what the job paid.

I slipped out my phone from my pocket and opened the calculator. After typing out the figure I had in mind, I showed it to her.

She stared at it and frowned. A full-on I-am-not-happy frown. The kind I'd expect from a toddler before they fell on the floor and threw a complete meltdown.

"You don't like what the job pays?" I could hardly believe I was asking that.

For a fake job to find a fake wife to partake in a very fake marriage, she was expecting a lot.

"No."

I looked over at Rock, who seemed just as baffled as me. He shrugged. "Why don't you type in what you expect to get paid to be Hamish's assistant?"

She plucked the phone from my hand a little too forcefully. The woman sure wasn't dainty.

After a few seconds of tapping at my phone, she held it up to me.

My eyes widened, and Rock leaned to the side to catch a glimpse. I knew he saw it because I heard him gasp before it turned into a coughing attack.

"This," I pointed to my phone, "this is what you expect to be paid for what will only be a few weeks of work? I have to get married soon, and once I find the woman to marry me, your job is over."

"Yes, I understand."

"Jami, I think that's a bit much for that type of job," Rock said after he managed to get his coughing under control.

I held out my hand, and Jami placed the phone in my palm. Gazing at those six figures, I was about to tell her

I'd get her sister Julia to help me. But then something that happened to Jami at the police station popped into my head.

"It's a deal. But you have to find me someone willing to marry me in three weeks."

"What?" Rock blurted out.

Jami put out her hand, and I grabbed it. I was surprised by her now firm handshake when the one I had in the kitchen with her was so limp.

I liked the woman. She was learning. Not just how to give a good handshake, but that she could trust me.

Jami was a surprise and knew what she wanted. Maybe she was the perfect woman for me… if only temporarily.

Chapter Eight

JAMI

"I have no idea what I'm doing," I blurted out to Julia as she sat at the kitchen table with her morning bowl of oatmeal and raisins.

It was Monday morning, a few days since the dinner party, and I was nervous.

"It's just cereal." Julia lifted the spoon to her mouth.

I shook my head. "Not my breakfast. I know how to eat cereal."

Did she actually believe I forgot how to eat?

I nibbled my lip. What my sister thought of me wasn't important right now. I had to focus. Today was the first day of my new job.

"Oh, I forgot to ask earlier, and I know you like advanced notice, but Nathan has another doctor appointment today. Laura said she can drive you two into town in her rental car before the appointment—"

"I can't." I stared at my toast with peanut butter and banana slices on it.

Julia's warm hand reached over for mine, and I tensed. She noticed and sighed. It just wasn't a good day. *Maybe I should call Hamish and tell him I changed my mind.*

"I know you are still upset about what happened on Friday with the car, but Laura is a lot better. I think she feels bad about getting mad at you. It wasn't your fault."

I twisted my fingers together, my attention turning to the French doors that led to the backyard. I saw Nancy pecking at something on the ground.

"It's not that. I understand why Laura was upset with me. I made a lot of mistakes that day, but I plan to change that. Make everything better."

There was silence. When I glanced up at my sister, her brow was wrinkled. It was the same look she gave Nathan when she suspected he pooped his diaper.

"And what is this plan of yours?"

I hadn't slept well the past two nights. The thought of this job with Hamish was scary. He seemed eager to hire me, yet he didn't know the real me.

There were things about me I knew would make him regret his decision. And that kept me up at night.

"I'm going to get the money to help pay for Laura's car."

"You don't need to do that, Jami—"

I shook my head. "Yes, I do. I shouldn't have been driving it. I don't even have a license. Why do you think I ended up in jail? I broke the law. Don't be mad at Officer Kolsti for taking me into the station—"

"I will never forgive him for that. I don't care what you say, Jami, he shouldn't have arrested you for that. It wasn't like you were some wanted criminal, and the cop got you on a suspended license. He could have helped you with Nathan and the car, but instead, he was power-tripping."

My sister's nostrils flared. There was no way to get through to her when she was angry.

Julia loved to hold grudges. Laura said it was Julia's favorite pastime. Currently, she was angry at her ex-boss Monty, and now Officer Kolsti. Once you upset her, it was almost impossible to get her to like you again. While I wasn't too worried about Officer Kolsti, I was worried about Monty. He was Rock's brother and a good guy—I knew it the moment I met him at Nathan's one-month-old birthday party.

"But I still shouldn't have been driving the car."

"Dad taught you how to drive. And if I'm being honest, I think out of all of us, you're the best driver."

"But I don't have a license."

She rolled her eyes. "That was Mom's fault. She was so worried you'd drive off and get lost. I was angry when she wouldn't let you get your driver's license."

I was hurt too. And now that I thought about it, the way my mom treated me like a child… like I was a toddler who would wonder off, I became angry.

As much as Julia stood up for me, she never treated me like an equal, either. I was never the sister who could take care of herself; I was the one everyone kept an eye on.

Maybe when I was little that was true, but not anymore.

"I got a *job*.".

Julia's eyes widened, and she lowered the spoonful of oatmeal before it got to her mouth.

"A job? When did this happen?"

There it was. Proof that I was still a child in her eyes. When Laura got a job as a chef at The Blue Spot, Julia jumped up and down, happy for her. The first word out of her mouth was congratulations.

But not for me. The crease between her eyes made me realize she was upset or disappointed—definitely not happy at all.

"At the dinner party on Friday." I sat up but kept glancing toward the backyard.

Julia tilted her head. "How can you get a job in our house during dinner? That doesn't make any sense... Wait, did Rock hire you?"

"No. Hamish."

That was when all the lines on my sister's face smoothed out. All my years learning how to read expressions was of no use right now as I couldn't tell what my sister was feeling. It was as if she felt nothing, but that wasn't like her. If there was one thing my sister always had, it was an emotion she was feeling.

"Hamish?" she asked before getting up from the kitchen chair. The soft thudding sound of the chair's wood legs gliding across the floor always sent a shiver up my spine.

"Yes. You like him. You told me that. And he's good friends with Rock. In fact, Rock told me about the job."

My sister walked to the refrigerator and pulled out some milk. After grabbing a glass from the cupboard, she filled it up and quickly threw back the drink.

"Alcohol works much better than milk. Damn this breastfeeding," my sister mumbled. "What exactly, and be as specific as possible, does this job entail?" She set the glass down on the counter and let out a loud burp. "Excuse me." She gave a half-smile.

"I am in charge of finding him a wife. Well, a woman to marry to become his wife."

My sister frowned. "I really want something to drink."

"Have some more milk." I waved at her glass.

She shook her head. "Not that type of drink."

Julia took a deep breath and plastered on a grin. It was fake; I knew her real smiles, and this wasn't it. She came and sat next to me.

"Jami, I get that you haven't had a job before. And you've graduated college and want to run on out there to start working. But having been around Hamish more than you, I think I have a pretty good idea what sort of person he is."

I waited for my sister to continue, but she just reached out for my hand and stared at me.

"Okay…"

"You understand what I'm saying, Jami?"

"No."

And what she did next would normally make me question if I was as smart as her. I'd normally wonder if I was strong enough to succeed at anything.

But not this time. This time when my sister let out a small sigh and the corner of her lips pinched down—the disappointment clear on her face—I didn't go running for Nancy.

"It means that Hamish is spoiled. He's the type of guy who's had everything and everyone handed to him on a platinum platter. He's wealthy and good-looking, and he knows it."

The more she spoke, the more my heart rate picked up. In her opinion, not only could I not handle a job, but my choice of boss was terrible too.

"And? He's not allowed to ever hire people? Is he bad at money?"

"No, but that's not—"

"Have you known him to hire terrible people? Workers who are bad at their job."

Her eyes scanned the room as if looking for something before they drifted to the floor. "Uh, no, but that doesn't mean he won't—"

"Julia, I am a grown woman. I managed to get a bachelor's degree in four years and didn't fall victim to all the terrible things you warned me about before I went off to university. Yet, despite all that, you think I can't hold down a job."

She was silent. Too quiet. My sister sat there looking at her fingernails. It was strange. Julia always had something to say, and now, nothing.

She cleared her throat after a minute. "You're right, Jami. I'm sorry. It's just hard, ya know? You've always been my little sister. The baby of the family. The one I wanted to protect from the harsh world. And now you are all grown up and got yourself a job. Congratulations." She scooted closer in the chair and threw her arm around my shoulder, giving me a side hug.

"I'm not a baby, and I haven't been a baby for almost two decades."

She nodded. "I know. But I'm the oldest. It's my job to protect my sisters. Laura was always so studious and knew exactly what to do, so I felt like I could never help her. If anything, she protected me… or tried to. But you, Jami… I was ten when you were born. I loved being able to take care of you. And now, I can't do that anymore."

I never knew that was how my sister saw it—that it was her job. I thought it was because she didn't believe in me.

"But you have Nathan."

She gave a hard laugh. "And one day he'll grow up and not need me either."

"He'll always need his mom, and I'll always need my big sister."

That brought a genuine smile to Julia's face.

"I need your help right now. I start this morning, and I don't know what to do. How should I dress?"

The smile grew. "Now that, I can help you with. You'll be working for a billionaire, so you want to dress in business attire, not office casual. Now, I know you said you're to find him a wife, but was that real? Maybe he was joking about that part."

"No, he wasn't. He specifically needs me to find him a bride in three weeks."

Her nose flared. "*Three weeks*?"

"He needs to marry. So, it will be my job to find the perfect wife for him."

She glanced around, then got up and began looking in drawers and on top of the refrigerator.

"Where is it?" Julia asked while continuing to look for something.

"What?"

"The hidden camera. James put you up to this, didn't he?" Then she stepped to the middle of the kitchen and raised her voice. "Ha, ha. Very funny, Jokin' James. Thought you could trick me, but I'm on to you."

James is Rock's youngest brother. His VidTube channel was called Jokin' James. He played pranks and did ridiculous stunts on the show. I used to watch it a few years ago, but not anymore.

I got up to help my sister find the camera. "I haven't seen him in a while. Did he tell you he planned to do a video here?"

"No." She came over to me, her arms folded. "You two set this up. The finding-Hamish-a-bride thing is a joke, right?"

"No. Why do you keep thinking it's a joke? It's my job."

She held up her hands and took a step back. "That's enough, Jami. This isn't funny. I cannot believe Rock would ask you to do a job like this. And what's more unbelievable is that Hamish Blackwell is even *considering* marriage. And to someone he doesn't know."

"I thought it was a big task too. That's why I asked for over a hundred thousand dollars for my pay."

Julia gasped. "The fu— No. Absolutely not." She shook her head and waved her hands in front of me.

I couldn't understand what she was objecting to. I may not have held down a job before, but I knew enough that six figures was a lot of money.

"No to the money?"

She stopped and put her hands on her hips. "No to everything, Jami. Everything. Why would a billionaire pay you one hundred thousand dollars to find him a wife? That sounds super sketchy."

"The job only lasts three weeks. I don't think that's enough time to do any harm to me—"

"And that's the other sketchy part about this. Three weeks to meet and marry a woman he's never met?" She put her hand on her forehead and paced around the small kitchen island.

Julia nearly walked into me when she came around, but I managed to step aside in time. I glanced at the clock on the microwave and realized I was about to be late.

"Look, Julia, you may not like the job, but it pays well —"

"That's an understatement," she said with a snort.

"And it's only three weeks. Just long enough for me to learn the skills I need to work another job. Like you mentioned, I have never had a job before, so this is perfect. Three weeks of training, and then I can find a more permanent job."

She stopped walking and took a breath. After a moment, she turned toward me.

"You know what? You're right. Maybe I'm just overreacting. You're my little sister, and this is your first job. Sure, what he's asking for is crazy, but from what I've learned from Hamish, he's a bit wild. And it is a good deal of money."

She walked over to me and gave me a hug. I was tense at first but relaxed quickly because I knew my sister loved me. She wasn't judging me in a bad way but looking out for my best interests.

"This bride…" She pulled back to face me. "Does she have to look a certain way?"

I shook my head. "No, she just needs to be a virgin."

And that was when Julia started to scream.

Chapter Nine

HAMISH

"She's late." Jenner stood in the doorway of my dilapidated room at The Blue Spot.

The place reeked of mildew, and every few minutes I heard some creatures scurrying in the walls. Actually, inside the walls. After hours of barely any sleep last night, I began to bang on the walls whenever I heard the critters.

I realized my mistake quickly as that seemed to egg them on. Instead of stopping, they just increased their movements, and I was sure they had found some friends to help them in their nightly exercise.

"Good. I'm tired and need more sleep. Please ask Rock if there are any rooms available. At this point, I'd sleep on the kitchen floor instead of this room."

Jenner waved down the hall. "Pick another room. There has to be at least ten here."

I sat up on the bed, which gave out a loud squeak of metal contorting under my weight.

"I've done that already. I have tried to sleep in every room, including the side of the hall Rock warned me against, but the animals… There are so many animals living in this building. Do you realize that? This is supposed to be an exclusive resort catering to the elite, and woodland creatures thought this was the best place to camp out for the autumn."

"I know this isn't the best situation for you—"

"Isn't the best?" I stood and became dizzy. I swayed a bit before the wooziness went away. "This needs to be condemned. I am sure I will get some illness living in this moldy, rodent-infested place. How did Rock get the inspector to sign off on the resort with this part of the building not fixed?"

"Easy." A deep voice came up behind Jenner. *Rock*. "This building isn't actually part of the rest of the resort. It was built separately from the building, so the inspector signed off on the resort, but not this part."

"If you don't plan to fix it, then tear it down."

I couldn't believe I was arguing about demolishing a building. Normally, I loved old architecture and wanted old buildings restored. But after living in a rundown, one-hundred-year-old building, I was all for burning it to the ground.

"It will be fixed. The builders were delayed and can't come until next week."

I walked over to the doorway and pushed past Jenner. Pointing my finger into Rock's chest, I said, "Then throw more money at them. The builders will come today, for a price. This needs to be fixed immediately."

"I think you need something to eat," Rock said as he wrapped his fingers around my hand and removed my finger from his chest.

"And coffee. God, I have never needed coffee so much in my life. And I once stayed up twenty-four hours to experience the northern lights in Iceland on the winter solstice."

"Then it's perfect we have the best coffee around." Rock winked at me.

I frowned. "Never wink at me again."

His eyes widened. "You do it all the time."

"Yes, but when I do it, people swoon. When you do it, you look like a robot trying to pass as a human."

"He is cranky when he doesn't get much sleep," Jenner added his two cents that no one asked for.

"Then you'll be happy to know I secured you a room in the main part of the resort."

My knees almost buckled, and I had to grab on to Rock to hold myself up. "Oh, thank god. Anything. Even if it's only five feet by five feet, I'll take it."

Rock placed his hand on my shoulder while Jenner gently nudged the other, and I found myself being guided down the hallway.

"Even better than that. It's a suite. Complete with a kitchenette, balcony, California king-sized bed, and walk-in shower." Rock pushed against my shoulder as my body leaned on him a little too much.

"I love you, Rock. Have I ever told you that? It's too bad you're not a twenty-one-year-old virgin because I'd get down on one knee and propose to you right now if I could."

Jenner chuckled.

I was serious. Anyone who got me out of that hovel should be awarded the Nobel Prize.

We came to the door that led to the main building, and as I reached for the handle with glee, someone stopped me.

I glanced over to discover the man I wanted to marry just moments ago was holding me back. I felt betrayed. Like he held a bacon maple donut in front of me but refused to let me have it.

"Why are we stopping? I've almost escaped this dungeon."

"You know how last week you were wanted for murder?" Rock asked.

"Yes. It was a misunderstanding, obviously. But I agreed to hide out here until it was resolved."

Jenner groaned. He only ever made that noise when something bad was about to happen. But what could be worse than being wanted for murder and then being forced to stay in a decaying building?

"Dick is here," Rock said, or perhaps it was Jenner. My ears began to vibrate once Dick's name was uttered, and I couldn't tell who was speaking.

"Here? In Castle Ridge?"

Jenner nodded while Rock rubbed the back of his neck.

"Okay, well then, it's good I'm hiding at your resort. I just won't leave the resort, like we planned."

The last thing I wanted was to run into Dick. I was sure he was eager to let the press and anyone who would listen know where I was located. He lived to make my life hell.

"He's actually at the resort… staying in one of the rooms." Rock glanced at the ceiling as he explained how he had backstabbed me.

I took a step back, holding on to the wall for support. "You're telling me you let that weasel into this place? I thought we were friends."

"We are, Hamish. It's just that I—"

"Money." I frowned and gazed at Rock in disgust. "That's all this is... just money to you. You saw dollar signs, and you had no problem letting him in."

Rock grabbed my shoulders and pulled me to face him. "Hamish, you're tired. I get it. You're under a lot of stress, and having to stay in this part of the resort probably wasn't great."

I snorted. My hand flew to my mouth in shock. I had never snorted in my life. *God, what was happening to me?*

"The reason I let your cousin stay at The Blue Spot is, if I refused him, he'd be suspicious. And knowing Dick, he'd find a way into the place just to hunt you down. But if I let him in, he's less likely to suspect you're staying here."

I stood there for a moment as the words sank in. Ugh, my brain was just not working properly today.

"That makes sense," I admitted slowly. "I'm sorry."

That sounded reasonable. It wasn't great, but it was a thousand times better than staying in the squirrel motel for the past two nights.

Rock shared a look with Jenner before lifting a black duffel bag from the floor. "You'll also need to wear what is in this bag. Wig and all."

"Wig?" I plucked the bag from Rock and opened the zipper. The first thing I pulled out was a bright pink dress.

"Are those... women's heels?" I picked one and held it up.

"I believe they are called stilettos," Jenner corrected me.

"Really? Please educate me on all the pieces of clothing I'm supposed to wear." I glared at my lawyer.

"Look, Hamish, I'm not doing this to humiliate you," Rock started.

"Are you sure? Because given my height and my overgrown five o'clock shadow, I'd say not one of your guests is going to mistake me for a woman."

I dropped the shoe to the ground and rummaged through the bag.

"Jewelry? Come on! This is ridiculous." I held up the gold necklace.

"Yes, if a guest walks right up to you, it's going to be obvious you are a man in women's clothing. Not that there's anything wrong with that. And that's the thing. People are much more accepting of how others dress and that sort of thing—"

"Rock," I grabbed his shoulder, "I get that, but look at me. If I wore this, I would look like a lumberjack in a hot pink dress, scruff and all. If you want to sneak me to my room and not draw attention to myself, then this is the worst possible idea you could have picked."

"I told you to go for the navy dress. Pink is too eye-catching," Jenner murmured.

"Or, and let's think about this for a moment, you could give me clothes for a man."

"But if we got you a suit, people would recognize you. I don't think I've ever seen you out of a suit. Even when we went skiing, you wore a suit around the lodge." Rock waved his hand up and down my body.

He was right. What else could I do but wear a dress and heels… I mean, stilettos? They were right. If I wore a suit, a few people would recognize me, or worse, Dick would find me.

"If it's all we have," I groaned. "Once I get to my suite, I can focus on finding a bride so I can inherit my grandfather's money and make sure my cousin Dick, that jerk, doesn't get a cent. That will make me happy."

Right at that moment, the door to the main part of the resort started to open. Both Rock and I stumbled back, but Jenner managed to step out of the way in time.

"Hey, who said you could come back here—" Rock raised his voice until he saw who opened the door.

"I was directed here by Mia, your assistant. Was I to wait in your office?" Jami asked.

Out of habit, my eyes slipped down her body. I knew I hired her to work for me, and normally, once someone was an employee, it was completely business. Unfortunately, that was going to be difficult with Jami.

She wore a body-hugging gray dress with an equally snug black blazer. And her dark heels made her legs look a mile long, even though she barely came up to my neck. I never thought office attire could be so sexy.

"No, sorry, Jami. I thought you were a lost hotel guest. This place is off-limits to them." Rock gave her a soft smile as his eyes drifted down. It wasn't in a I'm-checking-out-my-girlfriend's-sister sort of way, more like in a parental disapproving way.

"I didn't realize you owned heels or a dress or a blazer," Rock said through gritted teeth.

"I don't. Julia let me borrow some of her clothes until I can get things for myself. I hope this is appropriate." She was twisting her fingers together.

"Uh, it's okay for now. But maybe I'll take you shopping during lunch," Rock added.

I smiled down at her. "I think you look perfect."

She furrowed her brow. "Perfectionism is a belief that some think can be attained, but in reality, the human body is incapable of perfection in anything."

I blinked, and Jenner glanced over at me with a questioning look.

I cleared my throat and said, "Good to know. Now, maybe you can help us, Jami. I need to sneak out of here and up to my room on the…"

"Fourth floor," Rock said.

"Huh. I didn't realize this place had a fourth floor. Okay. Well, I need to get to my room without anyone recognizing me. Rock brought me a dress and a wig to change into, to pass me off as a woman. But with my build and facial hair, I don't think that's going to work."

She nodded, so I continued, "And I would prefer to dress like a man. But I'm known for always wearing a suit. So, you can see our conundrum. What do you think?"

The way she gazed up and down my body sent a shiver up my spine. Once her eyes met mine, she cleared her throat and turned her attention to the other men. "You can still dress like a man."

"But then I could be recognized—"

"Wear jeans and a flannel shirt. That's what a lot of guys in this town wear. Maybe the guests will think you're from town."

My hand went to my forehead. "Why didn't we think of that?"

It was one of those things that was so obvious, yet it didn't come to me.

An even bigger smile curled my lips. "And that's why I hired you. You know this place better than any of us. Now, help Rock find some jeans and a flannel, and we can start looking for my bride."

Although, I believed I already found her.

Chapter Ten

JAMI

"How is your first day going?" Laura grinned as she slipped into the chair opposite me.

I was seated at a dining table in her restaurant. She was head chef at The Blue Chip, The Blue Spot's five-star restaurant.

I smoothed out the white tablecloth, noticing a crumb left behind from a previous diner. "How did you find out I was working here?" I had only told Julia, so maybe she called Laura this morning.

"My boyfriend is the owner." She waved her hands around the room. "Anything that happens here, I know about it."

"Oh."

"I think this is great." She reached across the table and patted my hand lightly. "You're doing better than me at your age. My first job out of culinary school was a dishwasher at an Italian chain restaurant. The pay was crap; the work was exhausting, and the manager was a D-bag."

"I'm not tired, so I think it's a good day."

Laura nodded. "So tell me more. Is Hamish Blackwell as dashing as a boss as he was at dinner on Friday?"

I had to ponder what she asked. When it came to anything regarding romance and dating and relationships with the opposite sex, I was clueless. I knew what she was asking when she called him dashing, but I also knew it had to do with romance. Based on what Julia told me earlier today and how Laura was reacting, I guessed a lot of women were attracted to Hamish.

I could understand that. He was very handsome, but I also knew that looks meant nothing. Someone could be the most beautiful person in the world while also being the biggest jerk.

But Hamish had been nice to me from the moment I met him. I guess that was why I was happy when he offered me the job.

I had been worried about finding a job once I graduated, unsure how I would handle having to deal with so many people. Being comfortable enough around lots of people or strangers was what I struggled with the most. It wasn't about the work; I knew I could handle that easily. As my father always told me, I was a quick learner.

But having witnessed Laura work in the kitchen with so many different people making noises and yelling out questions all day, I shuddered just thinking about it.

But it was quiet with Hamish. And the only other people I needed to interact with were Rock—whom I already knew—and Jenner, who was Hamish's lawyer. I was getting used to Jenner.

"I guess." I shrugged.

"What she meant to say was, yes, Hamish has always been and will always be dashing," Hamish said from behind me.

I gasped. I hadn't realized he was there.

"I thought you were going to have lunch in your suite?" I gazed around the empty dining room. "You're in hiding."

Hamish waved his hand toward me. "Now why would I want to eat alone when I can sit at a table with the two most lovely and beautiful women in the world?"

Laura's cheeks turned pink, and she giggled. I tilted my head. Usually her laugh was hearty, but in front of Hamish, she sounded like a little girl.

"You're sweet. Jami is lucky to have a boss as nice as you."

Hamish shook his head. "No, I'm the lucky one. To find the perfect assistant on such short notice, and at such a steal." He winked at me.

Oh no. I wish people would stop winking. What did it even mean?

"A steal? Jami, you'll have to tell me later how much he pays you. I could help you negotiate more." My sister winked at me too.

Why was everyone winking? Heat ran up my neck, and I knew I was sweating. I pulled at the top of the tight dress I was wearing. I couldn't understand how Julia wore these clothes—they were so uncomfortable. And the shoes... I didn't think I had ever fallen so much in my life as I had in the past several hours.

"He's paying me a hundred and eight thousand dollars."

Laura's eyes widened. And while Hamish appeared not to move, I noticed his nostrils flared for a few seconds.

Laura shook her head. "I think I misheard you. It sounded like you said a hundred and eight thousand dollars. From what Rock told me, it's only three weeks' worth of work. Did you maybe mean just eight thousand?"

"No. One hundred and eight thousand. And yes, it is only for three weeks."

All the happiness in my sister's face melted away, and she turned to Hamish. "And what exactly is Mr. Blackwell having you do for all that money?" Laura stared at Hamish while she spoke to me.

"Oh, you know, just typical assistant stuff—" Hamish started to say before I cut him off.

"Find him a bride. A twenty-one-year-old virgin bride."

There was silence. Laura had the same look on her face that Julia had this morning when I first told her.

Laura glared at Hamish, and the more she glared at him, the more Hamish gazed around the restaurant. It was like he was taking in everything but my sister and me.

"Isn't it such a coincidence that Jami here also happens to be twenty-one years old," Laura said, refusing to take her eyes off Hamish.

"And a virgin," I added, and that was when Hamish shook his head, waving his hands at me. "I told him that in jail."

"Oh god," Hamish groaned and covered his face with his hands.

Laura leaned forward and grabbed his wrist, yanking his hand away from his face.

"You listen here, Mr. Billions. Don't think for one second that you can flash that perfectly white smile at me, and I won't notice you taking advantage of my sister. If I even suspect you hired her because you actually wanted her to be your bride in this sick, spoiled-little-rich-boy fantasy of yours, then there will be another person at this table wanted for murder. You got me?" she gritted.

"Wow, you've got a strong grip there." Hamish winced.

"Answer me."

Hamish nodded. "Yes, I got you." My sister released his hand but continued to glare. "There is a legitimate reason, not a fantasy. Trust me, I never date young, inexperienced women. I like a woman who knows how to pleasure me in the bedroom... Uh, I mean, someone I can have a mature conversation with." Hamish swallowed rather loudly while my sister refused to take her eyes off him.

"It's for an inheritance, Laura. It's in his grandfather's will that he marry a twenty-one-year-old virgin by his thirtieth birthday."

Hamish pointed at me. "See. Everything she told you is true. If you're mad at anyone, be mad at my ridiculously old-fashioned, horrible grandfather."

Laura sat back in her seat and folded her arms. "So, one of the richest men in the country needs more money from a will. Because if you don't get it, you'll only be as rich as you are now." She nodded with a frown. "Why didn't you say so? That sounds perfectly reasonable."

"Then why are you frowning?" I asked.

"Because I'm being sarcastic, Jami. A billionaire does not need any more money, not even a penny. Any wealthy person who tells you otherwise is a greedy liar. And that's who your boss is, a greedy liar."

What my sister said made sense. Hamish didn't need more money. But why was he going through with this if he didn't need the money?

"It's complicated," Hamish said while running his fingers through his thick blond hair.

"No, it's not." Laura sat up and leaned toward Hamish again. "That's what wealthy people do. The moment money is involved, it's suddenly complicated, something us mere *peasants* would never understand. The truth is, you're rich, and that's not enough for you. You think you need to be richer. So much so, you're willing to screw up some young woman's life just to get that money."

The more Laura spoke, the more I realized I might have made a terrible mistake. Would I be contributing to hurting a woman because of Hamish's greed? Six figures was a lot of money, especially for three weeks' worth of work, but not at the expense of someone's life.

"She's right. You don't need that money."

I couldn't help but feel hurt by the situation. He tricked me. Both my sisters had been right about Hamish. What seemed like the perfect first job for me was turning out of be the worst one I could ever get.

Hamish inhaled deeply and closed his eyes. When he opened them again, he turned his attention to me. His gray eyes glistened with something that made me feel even more confused. My heart pounded in my chest, but it was the heat that bloomed between my thighs that most concerned me.

The way Hamish stared at me, turned me on… He was my boss and, from what I was now learning about him, not a very good one. Despite that, I had the strongest urge to lean over and kiss him.

Oh god. Something was wrong with me.

"Both of you are correct. I don't need another cent. What I was planning to do with that money when I inherited it—"

"*If* you inherit it," my sister corrected him.

"Right, if I inherit the money, I plan to give it all to charity. The money was never the reason I wanted it."

"Really?" Laura asked.

"Yes, really. It's just something I felt I needed to do to make my grandfather happy. It was in his will for a reason. I know the man was old-fashioned and racist and sexist and just about every 'ist' that exists. But he also loved me and treated me kindly growing up. He's family, and in wealthy families like mine, heart is a rare thing to find. Like you mentioned, it's all about greed. My grandfather wasn't all about money; he loved his family. And besides, I only have to marry the woman for two months; that's it. Then we can have a quick divorce—one of the perks of being rich—and we can both go about our lives as usual."

My sister sat there silently.

"Maybe that's why Rock helped you," she finally said. "Part of my anger was about him helping you. I had planned to march into his office and tell him exactly how I felt about getting my sister this job. But I know taking care of family is really important to Rock. If what you said is true, then I can't really be mad at you for that."

"I can," I said, and all eyes turned toward me.

"Jami, I didn't know the whole story. I assumed the worst and was wrong. I get why you took the job now. And you're making a lot of money too."

But Hamish was wrong.

"Why did you just lie to my sister?" I asked him.

Hamish's eyes slid to Laura before quickly turning back to me. "I didn't lie to her—"

"Yes, you did. Why aren't you telling her the truth? And for that matter, why didn't you tell me everything when you offered me the job?"

He cleared his throat and sat up a little taller in his chair. "I told you exactly what the job entailed. What you would be required to do, and you had no problem with that, especially when I agreed to your six-figure payment."

"What are you talking about, Jami?" Laura leaned over, placing her hand on my arm, concern etched in the corner of her eyes.

"I heard you talking to Rock and Jenner this morning right before I opened the door. You had that bag of clothes in your hand, and everyone was surprised when I showed up, but Mia had directed me there. I heard you say you thought your cousin Dick was a jerk. That you'd be happy he wouldn't get a cent of the inheritance if you got married. You talk about loving family, but your cousin is family, and you are only doing this to hurt him."

"What?" Laura said rather loudly.

I glanced around and was surprised the restaurant was still empty. It was lunchtime; there should have been people in here.

"It's not what you think." Hamish started to rise from his chair as my sister stood.

"It's exactly what I think. Come on, Jami; we're going to talk to my soon-to-be ex-boyfriend."

I stood, but my stomach began to growl for food. As we walked away, I heard Hamish mumble, "Well, Grandfather, you must be laughing up there in heaven… or maybe down there in hell. You always knew how to screw over my life."

Chapter Eleven

HAMISH

I stared out at the gorgeous autumn view of the Blue Ridge Mountains; the leaves were turning an array of yellow, purple, and red. Turning back toward the flawlessly appointed suite I had been staying in the past two days, I felt unusual.

It was a feeling I had spent my life running from. I had never been one of those guys who refused to acknowledge his faults. We were all human. No matter how much money a person had in their bank account, words could still cut you deeper than any knife.

What Jami said to me at The Blue Chip on Monday felt like the sharpest blade.

And that feeling of loneliness I spent my money hiding from was back, and I was stuck in this fantastic room to face it.

"Cheer up. What, did someone die?" Jenner walked into the bedroom with coffee in a paper cup.

He held it out for me, but I waved it away. I was awake, even if I didn't want to be.

"My grandfather. Remember?"

He winced. "Right. Sorry. But you weren't that broken up about it when you originally found out. Why now?"

I hadn't lied to Laura. I did love my grandfather, and he always doted on me. He was also a terrible racist and sexist and all that. But like I said, he was family.

While I was glad he was at peace, I was also happy he no longer was living an angry, bitter life. And despite how I felt, I needed to get on with business—clear my name and seek out a bride, not necessarily in that order.

"It's the marriage. Is there any loophole you can find to get me out of it? Something. None of this feels right."

Jenner walked over to the edge of my bed—which was covered in a blue silk bedspread—and sat. He picked at the edge of the paper cup and shook his head.

"What do you think I've been doing since Friday? Every time I'm not with you, I'm making calls to other lawyers and rereading the will to find even the smallest grain of sand we might be able to fight in court. I've got nothing. Your grandfather had access to the best lawyers, and they made that will so tight, a nineteenth-century corset would be jealous."

I tilted my head. "Corset?"

"Don't judge me. I'm stressed, and when I'm stressed, I watch a lot of period dramas."

Never would I have expected that from my slick, city-loving lawyer, but you learn something new every day.

"Ugh. I feel like I am in the same spot I was in five days ago. Only, instead of a tiny cell in a small-town jail, I'm stuck in a luxurious suite."

"Hey, it could be worse. You could still be in the run-down rooms here."

I nodded. "That's true. I guess I blocked it out because it was so awful."

"I thought you hired that woman Jami?"

"That was two days ago. I didn't exactly tell her the truth as to why I wanted my grandfather's money, but she found out anyway. She seems to think I'm being spiteful to my cousin, and that's the only reason."

"You should be doing it out of spite. Dick is an asshole. And being a lawyer, I've met a whole lot of assholes in my day. But Dick… he's the king of assholes."

I sighed, grabbed the coffee from Jenner, and sat next to him on the bed. "Yes, but she doesn't know that. She's never met him."

"Ahh, I see. She just thinks you're being a greedy jerk."

"Why does everyone assume the worst of me? I thought people loved me, but something happened a week ago, and suddenly, I'm the worst person on Earth."

Jenner blinked before staring at me.

"What?"

"Hamish, do you remember what happened on Friday? You were arrested for murder. Most people don't like murderers."

I groaned, "I know, but I'm *not* a murderer. And the way people treated me before the whole might-be-a-murderer thing was the total opposite. People couldn't get enough of me. I can't believe everyone would turn on me so quickly."

I took a swig of the coffee and frowned. It was lukewarm, but I didn't care as I took another sip.

"You're a celebrity, not their next-door neighbor or their friend from high school. To them, you aren't human. And the fact that you have so much money makes you even less real. If you get hurt, they may spend two seconds on social media typing how sorry they are, but then they go about their day, not concerned about you at all."

"I know that. I don't personally know these people, but what about the ones I do know? Jami was nice; she was the first person I had ever met who didn't see dollar signs or something they could get from me. She seemed like a person who actually wanted to know me and not what I could do for her."

Jenner chuckled and placed his hand on my shoulder. "Is that why she asked for a hundred thousand dollars?"

My jaw tightened. I wasn't talking about that.

"Anyway, she was earnest, not shallow. I really did want her help."

Maybe a little bit more than help, but I knew legally, this was a tight rope I was walking. If I put the moves on Jami as my employee, I could easily be sued for all my grandfather's money and more.

I liked her, but I wasn't an idiot. Growing up with millions and billions, you learned early to understand the law.

"Maybe she was. I mean, she did walk away from all that money just because she thought you hated your cousin."

"See?" I shifted on the edge of the bed to face Jenner. "I told you. Even if she doesn't want to help me find a bride, I want her back. Just as an assistant while I'm here. I'd pay her the same amount."

Jenner watched me, and for a second, I thought he was about to say something. His mouth opened and closed a few times without a word uttered.

"Is something wrong?" I asked.

"You." He smirked. "You like her."

"Yes. Of course, I like her. I just said she was nice and earnest—"

"No, Hamish. You have a crush on her."

I narrowed my eyes and stood. "What am I, in high school? You know me better than that, Jenner. All I was saying is that she was nice, and I felt as if I could trust her. As you know, trust is hard to come by, especially in my world."

He got up and shook his head. "Call it trust if you want, but I do know you. And you have never spoken about a woman like that before."

I walked out of the bedroom to the kitchenette and poured the coffee down the sink. "The most I would ever think of Jami would be as a friend. Since I haven't known her very long, I can't call her that. She doesn't want anything to do with me, so I really can't even call her a friend. That's all I was saying."

"I'm your friend, and because of that, I will make it my business to get her back here."

Turning from the sink, I saw Jenner stand in the middle of the room, checking his phone.

"I see you still have your phone. That's almost an entire week without losing a phone. Is that a record?"

He shook his head. "No. And this is actually a new phone. I lost one on Monday. Just got this."

How could he be such a great lawyer and so lousy with phones?

I pointed at him. "Don't bribe Jami."

He put the phone in his pocket. "Not at all. Like you said, she's earnest. Money won't sway her. But I think I know what will…"

Jenner had that gleam in his eyes—the same one he had in courtrooms and seated at negotiation tables. That look told me he was about to win.

"Fine. But please, respect her wishes. The last thing I want is for her to think I'm tricking her."

Jenner strolled over and patted my arm. "I will, I promise. Have I ever lied to you before?"

"Yes—"

"Wait. Don't answer that."

Chapter Twelve

JAMI

"Don't worry. After what Laura told me on Monday about what Hamish said, I will make sure he doesn't take advantage of you again." Julia scanned Blue Beans as her fingers played with the handle of the white porcelain coffee cup in front of her.

We were seated in The Blue Spot's coffee shop, waiting for Hamish. This time, the place wasn't empty—not like The Blue Chip was on Monday. Most of the dark wooden tables were taken up by customers, sipping their coffee.

I asked Laura if that was normal for Monday lunchtime. She told me no. Hamish had the place cleared so no one would recognize him.

If that were true, then why wasn't Blue Beans cleared of people?

"Hello, ladies," a male voice came from behind.

I turned to discover Jenner, Hamish's lawyer.

"Where's Hamish?" I asked more eagerly than I had wanted.

"I hope I haven't kept you waiting?" Jenner ignored my question.

When I got a text to meet Hamish at Blue Beans this afternoon, I would be lying if I said a thrill hadn't gone up my spine.

Ever since I walked out of The Blue Chip on Monday, I hadn't been able to get Hamish out of my head. And every time I thought about him, that heat between my legs intensified.

Many times, I stuck my hands down my pants and imagined those molten gray eyes staring down at me.

But I didn't dare tell Laura or Julia what I thought. They hated him and kept reminding me that he was a bad guy.

But was he? The more I thought about it, the more I understood not liking all members of your family. I hated my uncle. He made fun of my mom and treated me like someone to pity.

"Not long," I said right as my sister said, "Yes."

Jenner's eyes bounced between both of us before he threw his head back with a chuckle. "Sisters." He shook his head and pulled out a dark wood chair, taking a seat.

Julia's eyes narrowed. She wasn't happy. And if Julia didn't like someone, she most likely never would.

"To answer your question, Jami," Jenner shifted to face me, "Hamish won't be coming. I know you're aware of why he can't be seen in public... with the murder investigation and all that." He laughed again.

I didn't like to call people weird because it wasn't nice to say. Some people just liked their own thing, and if someone couldn't understand that, then that was their problem. It never made a person weird.

But laughing at murder... well, that was strange.

Julia folded her arms and sat back. "Then why is Jami here?"

"I believe Jami has the wrong idea about Hamish. He isn't some greedy billionaire looking to hurt his family. He never wanted the money. In fact, when I first told him about the stipulation in his grandfather's will, he told me no. The last thing he wanted was to drag a stranger, a young woman, into his family's eccentricities."

"Eccentrici-what?" Julia asked.

"Eccentricities. It means being eccentric, odd behavior," I said.

"Okay, but even if I believe you... which I don't. But if I did, then why did he decide to go through with trying to marry a twenty-one-year-old virgin?" My sister lifted the cup of coffee to her lips and took a sip.

"As Jami rightly pointed out on Monday, it was to make sure his cousin didn't get the money."

My heart sank in my chest. I wanted to believe I was wrong—that it wasn't about spite. But it was. That wasn't a good enough reason to go through with it. I didn't like my uncle, but I would never marry someone for money because of it.

"That's petty," Julia said and then pursed her lips.

She wasn't wrong.

"If it had been anyone else besides Dick Kerry, I'd completely agree with you. But you've never met Dick. I'll just tell you that his name suits him."

Julia tapped her finger on the table. "Dick Kerry. Dick Kerry. Why does that name sound familiar?"

"Maybe you heard about one of his exploits. Like a few years ago, he visited a kid with cancer in the children's hospital in New York. Dick publicly promised to pay all his medical bills. Only, he never paid anything, and then he turned around and sued the parents for libel when they went on the local news, explaining they hadn't received any payment from him in the year since he promised."

My sister brought her hand up to her mouth. "Oh my god, that was him?"

It did seem like his first name was an apt description.

"Yes. He likes to try to sleep with other men's wives and girlfriends. He sees it as a sport, something to brag about if he wins. Oh, and he's married. I don't know if his wife turns a blind eye to it or is just that clueless, because he isn't subtle."

"That's terrible," I mumbled.

"Another reason he might be familiar to you is his best friend, Kodi Corradi."

Julia sat up in her seat. "He's the guy who had that sex dungeon. The police raided it a year ago and found a dozen women and men who had been kidnapped and tortured by him."

"Yes. He kidnapped those people, some of them just teenagers at the time, and then tortured them. Then he'd charge his wealthy friends to come over and do whatever they liked to the victims. And Dick was friends with him the whole time. Even stuck up for him when he was arrested, saying he was a 'good guy.'"

"Ugh." My sister looked like she was about to throw up.

"You're right. Dick Kerry is a terrible person," I said as the pain in my chest grew.

I didn't even know those people who were tortured, but my heart hurt thinking about what they had been through. How could anyone do that? And how could anyone want to be friends with someone so awful?

"So here we are." Jenner waved his hands at the table. "If Hamish doesn't marry this young woman—who has yet to be determined—then all the billions of dollars and property go to Dick Kerry. I wonder what he could do with all that money? Buy influence in D.C.? Perhaps fund campaigners to get people elected who would then help him crush the poor. I say crush the poor because I overhead him at a party once. He said that if he could, he would 'crush the poor.'"

"That motherfucker," Julia said, gritting her teeth.

"Hamish doesn't want or need his grandfather's wealth, but he will do anything to keep it out of Dick's hands." Jenner sat back and sighed.

We sat in silence for a few minutes, absorbing Jenner's words when a voice called out that I didn't recognize.

"Jenner? Jenner Cartwright, is that you?"

Jenner's mouth twitched as he sat up straight, peering over his shoulder. "Speak of the devil," he mumbled. "Dick. I'd say it was lovely to see you here, but it's not."

Dick smirked, but his dark brown eyes didn't stay on Jenner too long. They slid over to me and my sister and lingered.

"Always the joker, Jenner. I guess that's why my cousin keeps you around. He can't help but surround himself with goof-offs. Speaking of Hamish, I assume you're here because of him. Where is he?"

Dick finally settled his gaze on me. There was something in the way he watched me that gave me the feeling I was his prey. Like he was the wolf, and I was a small woodland creature, desperate to be invisible.

I didn't want to look at him anymore, so I stared at the table. Just him standing there had my heart racing, and not in a good way.

"Not here," Jenner lied.

"Come on, Jenner. We both know he murdered a poor innocent construction worker. I've reached out to his family and offered to pay for the funeral myself because it breaks my heart to know that a person from my family would do such a horrible thing."

"I didn't realize you even had a heart to break," Jenner said.

I smiled. I liked Jenner.

"Are you *actually* going to pay for the funeral expenses, or are you going to stiff them like you did that dying child's family?" Julia asked.

I glanced up to find my sister glaring at Dick.

"I have no idea what you are talking about, nor do I associate with people lesser than me." Dick frowned at my sister.

"*Lesser*?" Julia raised her voice and stood.

Jenner reached over and grabbed her wrist, shaking his head. "He's not worth it."

Julia's nose flared. I could tell she wasn't happy, but she sat back in her chair anyway.

"Now, this beautiful creature, I'll talk to. What's your name?" Dick came over to my side and leaned down until I could feel his hot breath skimming my ear.

My stomach churned, and I worried I might throw up my lunch.

"She's none of your business, Dick."

"I tell you every time, it's Richard. Call me Richard."

"I would, but you just seem more like a Dick to me."

I couldn't help but laugh.

"That's not funny," Dick said harshly. "You know, Jenner, the longer Hamish hides, the less time he has to fulfill the requirements Grandfather stated in his will. If he can't marry a twenty-one-year-old virgin by his birthday, then it looks like I get everything. I think that would make me the richest man in the US."

Jenner stood and faced Dick. "How did you find out about what Hamish had to do to get his grandfather's money?"

"Oh, come now, Jenner. I have friends in high places too. There are lots of things I know. Take this place, for instance... Did you know Hamish's best friend, Rock Diaz, is the owner of The Blue Spot? And I find it interesting that just last week, Hamish was bailed out of jail by you at the sheriff's station just down the road. I know he's here, and once I find him, well... let's just say no woman will agree to marry him."

I hated Dick. Not only had he done terrible things to innocent people, but he seemed to *enjoy* hurting people.

Growing up in this small mountain town, kids in school always made fun of me, told me I acted like a psycho. One even said he wouldn't be surprised if he discovered I was a serial killer one day because I had trouble looking people in the eye and didn't like to be touched. My ex said it.

Yet, guys like Dick constantly treated people horribly and got away with it. He could do whatever he wanted, say whatever he wanted, and never had to worry about people calling him out on it.

Maybe that was why I liked Jenner. In the past five minutes, Jenner let him know how much he hated Dick and didn't care what he thought.

Now I understood why Hamish had to marry. He was doing what he needed to keep that money from getting into this jerk's hands.

And that was why I stood, turned to Dick, and said, "That's not true. I've agreed to marry him."

Jenner grinned. I worried I made a terrible mistake when my sister gasped, but then I saw Dick's face. The way he ground his teeth and narrowed his eyes at me was all the reassurance I needed to know that marrying Hamish was the best decision of my life.

Chapter Thirteen

HAMISH

"You know you have a key too, Jenner. You don't need me to open the door for you," I said as I walked toward the door of the room I had been staying in for the past two days.

"But it's a surprise," Jenner's muffled voice carried through the door.

I rolled my eyes. "Okay." I reached for the knob and opened the door.

On the other side stood Jenner, and next to him, Jami.

My heart leaped. A smile burst forth on my face, and I didn't care if I looked like a buffoon.

Relief and joy flooded my veins at the sight of her. She was wearing jeans that hugged her hips perfectly and a white cotton blouse. Her hair was twisted in a thick blond braid. She seemed like the perfect model for this mountain town.

Beautiful. Fresh. Natural.

Jami was like no woman I had ever thought about kissing before, but right now, the only thing I wanted to do was cup her cheeks and pull her to my lips.

"Jami. It's lovely to see you again." I took a step back and waved her inside.

She seemed hesitant as she moved into the room. I was so enamored that I almost closed the door on Jenner.

"Hey. I'm here too." Jenner grabbed the door before it slammed in his face.

"Sorry. I forgot you were there."

Jenner chuckled. "Obviously."

I followed Jami farther into the room. She glanced around but appeared uneasy.

Was it because of me?

"Please, have a seat." I waved to the navy tufted couch near the large window.

She ignored me. Instead, she walked over to the window and stared at the beautiful view.

I glanced back at Jenner. "Does this mean she agreed to come work for me?"

Jenner's smile grew, and all at once, I felt relief.

"Better," he said.

Jami turned toward me. "I've agreed to marry you."

My eyes widened. The relief I felt moments ago pivoted to excitement. Despite my happiness, there was something tickling the back of my mind. Trepidation.

It was only for two months, I reminded myself.

"Marry? Really?"

I was stunned. My mind raced, wondering what made her change her mind.

Jenner. He did get that winning look in his eyes before he left earlier. He must have known what she wanted.

That man was getting a raise.

"Yes." Jenner caught me staring at him to continue, so he did. "We met someone down in the coffee shop. Dick."

"Oh shit." I rubbed my brow. "If he said anything to hurt you, I apologize. He's not a good man."

"Why are you apologizing? You didn't say those things."

I sighed and took a few steps closer to her. "You're right. But the thought of Dick even being in the same room as you is upsetting. I won't lie, he's not a good man."

"Yes, Jenner told me."

I turned to my lawyer.

"You'd be surprised what telling the truth can do, Hamish. There was no reason to hold that information back from Jami. And I knew Dick was here and always had coffee in the afternoon. Even if Jami didn't believe me, I knew if she met him, she'd realize why it was so important he never get the inheritance."

I glanced back at Jami. She was beautiful and sweet, but also young. And Laura's words really hit me in the gut.

"Jenner, would you mind giving us some time alone?"

His eyes shifted between us, and he winked. "Of course. I'll head over to see Rock."

I shook my head. It wasn't what he thought.

"Okay, I'll call you when I'm ready." I waited until Jenner left the room and closed the door behind him.

Jami was back at the window, staring at the view, so I strolled up beside her. "It's so beautiful here. Now I know why you live here."

"I live here because it's the only place I've ever known. There's no reason for me to leave. My sisters are here. My parents' house is here. They're retired and traveling the country, but they still come back for holidays."

"My dad's dead, but he owned a penthouse in New York City, so that's where I was raised. My mom…? I think the last time I checked, she was in India finding herself. I haven't seen her in years."

She blinked up at me. "That's terrible. I love my parents. They made mistakes, but even with that, they did it with love. Like… my problem with touching."

I turned to face her. "Touching?"

She shook her head, tucking a stray hair behind her ear. "Look, there's something you should know about me." She swallowed, clearly uncomfortable with what she was about to say.

"If you need some time, you can always—"

"No. I need to tell you. And I understand if you don't want to follow through with the marriage after you find out."

My head shot back. What could possibly be so terrible that I wouldn't want to marry this amazing woman?

She kept opening and closing her mouth, struggling to tell me her truth.

"I didn't think it would be this hard." She let out a soft chuckle. "I, uh… I have autism." Jami stood there not moving, just staring at my chest.

"Okay," I said.

I waited for her to keep going. I waited to find out whatever was upsetting her to the point of thinking I wouldn't want to be with her. There had to be more; it couldn't be that she had autism.

"So, if you want to back out of the marriage, I understand." A lonely tear slid down her face.

"That's it? Just that you have autism?"

Her eyes slid back and forth, but other than that, she remained still. "Yes."

I moved over to the couch and sat. She really believed I wouldn't want anything to do with her once I discovered this about her.

"Well, then the marriage is off," I said sarcastically and waved my hands in the air.

She nodded. "Yes, I understand." Jami turned and headed toward the door.

"No. Please, stop." I ran around her to block her exit. "I mean, you can go if you really want to, but I was only joking when I said the marriage is off. I was being sarcastic."

She frowned, and I'd be lying if I said it wasn't adorable.

"I don't always get sarcasm... My sister, Julia, was very sarcastic when I was younger, but she learned not to be that way with me because I didn't understand. I'm sorry."

I reached out to touch her arm, and she flinched. *Right. She doesn't like to be touched.*

"Don't be sorry for who you are, Jami. You're sweet and funny and beautiful, and I could keep going, but I don't want to creep you out."

Damn. Now I probably had disturbed her just by saying that out loud.

"You aren't creepy."

"I realize what I'm asking you to do isn't normal. And I will agree to give you whatever you want once the divorce is finalized. But please, don't think because you have autism that I wouldn't like you or even want to marry you. Did someone tell you that?"

She lowered her gaze to the floor, her arms wrapped around her torso. It took her a moment, but she finally spoke.

"All my life, before I was diagnosed, kids called me weird or crazy. Then afterward, they called me stupid and said that no one would ever want to marry me. Even some parents told my mother they felt sorry for her since she had to raise a child who would never have anything to contribute to society."

I rubbed at the pain in my chest. All I wanted to do was wrap my arms around her and pull her to me. Not because she was sexy, but because she believed all those awful things people told her.

I lowered my head, trying my best to catch her sad gaze. "You know what they said was a lie, right, Jami?"

Her brown eyes flickered to mine for a moment before slipping down once again. "That's what Julia told me," she whispered.

What I didn't understand was how she found out what parents told her mom. "Why would your mom tell you what other parents said about you?"

That made me the angriest—that her own mother would tell her that. She didn't need to hear it. Some say honesty is always the best policy, but not when its only purpose was to hurt people. And to do it to her own child...? I would never understand that.

"She didn't tell me. I was standing next to her when parents would say that to her. I think they thought I couldn't understand them, but I did."

My head fell back as I let out a sigh and my eyes began to burn. Fuck them. I was so angry, I wanted to punch the wall. But I knew that would scare Jami, so I took deep breaths instead.

I lifted my head and said, "Okay, but they were wrong. I don't care what anyone says, those people were just mean and ignorant. They were blind to all the beautiful gifts you give every day. Is it okay if I hold your hand?"

The urge to touch her was eating away at me. I'd take anything she gave, even the smallest touch.

"Okay." She held out her hand as if I was about to shake it, but I clasped it gently between both of mine. Her hand stiffened immediately, but once my thumb slowly drifted back and forth over the back of her hand, I felt her relax.

"Is this okay?"

She nodded. Her eyes were fixed on what I was doing to her. Jami's skin was decadently soft. Heat shimmied down to my cock, and it twitched to life.

My god, I was becoming aroused just by holding her hand. I knew I had to keep this thing with Jami platonic, but damn if I didn't want to move up her arm and pull her close.

"It's strange."

She didn't like it, and that was disappointing. Here I was getting turned on just by rubbing her hand, and she hated it.

"What's strange?" I asked reluctantly.

"I'm just standing here, not even moving, but my heart is beating so fast in my chest. It feels like it does after I run."

My lips curled, and I took the tiniest step forward. "Mmm. Mine too."

She licked her lips. My new purpose in life was to watch her do that a thousand times.

"Do you want me to stop?" My eyes closed as I said a silent prayer for her to say no.

"No. It feels good."

"Okay. I'll continue." I flipped her hand over and began to rub her palm. Her nose flared with a sharp intake of breath.

The way Jami reacted to my touch was addictive. I wanted more, so I took it.

My fingers slid up until I drew circles over the pale blue lines of her wrist. She made a noise; it was faint, but just enough for me to realize I had made her moan.

"Is this alright?" I asked as I lifted her other hand, mimicking the touch.

"Yes." Her word sounded breathless.

There was something I had wanted to ask her since she first walked into my room. I knew it was taking it too far, but the way my cock throbbed, there was no going back.

"Jami, have you ever been kissed?"

Her head lifted, and she stared up at me with glazed eyes. Her pouty lips parted for her to whisper, "Yes."

I was surprised by her answer. Not because I felt she was sheltered, but because she admitted to having a problem with being touched.

"Did you like it?"

She shook her head. "I had a boyfriend in college, though we didn't date very long. But whenever he kissed me, it felt rough, and I always had to wipe my mouth after. I think he may have had a drooling problem."

I snickered.

"Then he did it wrong." I shrugged. "Most young men don't know what they're doing. It takes time to get things right, to learn what your partner enjoys."

"Oh?" Her voice cracked.

It was adorable.

"Can I kiss you? You don't have to say yes, but it's tradition after a man and woman are married for him to kiss the bride. Maybe we should try it and see how it goes?"

I didn't really think we should practice before the wedding, I just wanted to kiss Jami.

She frowned, and I thought she was about to say no.

"That does sound like a good idea... Maybe we should try."

The corner of my lips curved. She said yes.

I lowered my head to hers before she changed her mind. Inhaling, my nose filled with the scent of lilac. I let my hand drift up her arm. There were goose pimples dotting her flesh. My fingers slipped around her neck, her thick braid skimming the back of my hand.

I couldn't help the groan that escaped my throat as my lips drifted across hers. Jami was so soft, and as much as I wanted to pull her tight to my body, I knew it was time to be gentle.

My lips lingered on hers for a moment before I imprinted the kiss. Tilting my head back, I watched her. Her eyes scanned mine before falling to my mouth.

She wanted more.

I was happy to gift her with whatever she desired. My mouth lowered onto hers, but this time, I wasn't as gentle.

My mouth dotted hers with kisses, each firmer than the last. When she reached up and cupped my cheek, I took a risk and wrapped my arms around her.

She didn't hesitate or back away, so I pulled her closer. That was when she melted. Her tits rubbed against my abdomen. My fingers curled into her hip to stop myself from reaching up and cupping her breast. Everything about her was decadent, and it was difficult not to indulge.

When her lips parted, I took that as an invitation, and my tongue slipped inside. Her hands fell, her fingers digging into my shoulders, and I knew she enjoyed all the risks I had taken.

My cock was at full attention, and if I let this continue, I feared Jami would regret agreeing to the kiss. I pulled back and watched her gasp for air. My mouth curved as I noticed her glasses were askew.

"Why, uh… why did you stop?" she asked between breaths.

I reached up and slid my thumb across her bottom lip. "Because it was only supposed to be a kiss. If we kept it up, it would have turned into so much more."

She gave a devious smile. "So?"

I lowered my head and kissed her forehead before taking a step back. I needed to control myself around her.

"If you actually want to do more with me, then we would have to be married. Remember, you have to be a virgin when we marry."

I couldn't believe I was saying that. Never in my life did I believe I'd be uttering those words or stopping a beautiful woman from wanting to take kissing to the next level.

My grandfather had a twisted sense of love.

She took a step forward and placed her hand on my chest. "Okay, then we can get married today."

"Today?" I asked, and my voice went up an octave. "Uh, we still need the marriage license and someone who can legally marry us, like a minister or the justice of the peace. That may take a while."

"Hmm." She tapped her chin. "Can Jenner help us make that happen?"

"Of course, but—"

"Then tell him I want to get married as soon as possible. Then we can pick up where we left off." She smiled and winked before heading to the front door to leave.

I got what I wanted. A twenty-one-year-old virgin had agreed to marry me. She was sexy and smart, and as I had suspected, she was an incredible kisser.

But as I stood there watching her sculpted ass sway as the door closed behind her, I worried. Marriage was a big step to take just because of a hot kiss.

Chapter Fourteen

JAMI

"Hey, Julia, can I ask you something?" I asked my sister as she sat on the back deck chair, breastfeeding Nathan.

"Shoot." Her thumb gently rubbed his cheek.

"Would you be my maid of honor at my wedding?"

Her eyes widened, and her hand fell from Nathan's face. "So, you're going through with it? You plan to marry Hamish?"

While Julia first agreed with me about marrying Hamish after meeting Dick, she had since changed her mind. Most of her hesitation was about Hamish. She liked him, but not enough for me to marry, even if it was only temporary.

"Yes, even more so now." I felt the heat creep up my neck to my cheeks.

Every time I thought about Hamish, I kept imagining his lips on mine. He was a great kisser.

In the past, I never knew why my sisters said they loved kissing men, but now I understood. My ex was terrible at it, and I had thought all kissing was like that. Boy, was I wrong.

The way his cool gray eyes looked at me caused heat to explode between my legs.

"Even more now? Why now?"

I didn't like the look she was giving me—it was her judgmental expression. She mostly used it on Laura, but occasionally, and more so now, she'd throw it my way.

"We kissed."

She tried to shift in the chair to face me, but it was difficult with Nathan in her arms. "Okay. Did you kiss him, or did he kiss you?"

"Uh, why does that matter?"

"Oh, it matters. Look, Jami, I still am having a hard time trusting Hamish. He may say these great things, but with all his money, he can say anything he wants and not get in trouble for it."

I was getting tired of Julia assuming the worst from Hamish. She said she knew him, but I didn't believe it.

"He kissed me. But he asked first, and I agreed."

She rolled her eyes. *What was her problem?*

Julia mumbled something, and I didn't even have to hear what she said. I knew it was another bad comment about Hamish.

I stood. "Forget I asked. I'll go ask Laura. And if you hate him that much, then you don't even have to come to the wedding."

My jaw tightened, and normally I would go get Nancy when I got this angry, but all I could think about was running to Hamish. I hadn't seen him much in the past two days, and when I did, Jenner or Rock was always there.

But when I did see him, I let him hold my hand, which relaxed me.

"Jami, I didn't mean—"

I stopped before I got to the door leading into the house and turned back toward Julia. She had taken Nathan off her breast and was adjusting her nursing bra.

"Yes, you did. You meant every word you said about Hamish. Whether you like it or not, I am a grown woman who is marrying a man you don't like. Tough. If I am making a mistake marrying him, then it is my mistake to make."

She placed Nathan in his little basket and stood. "I know, and I'm sorry if I hurt you. But I'm your sister. I only want what's best for you."

"Then you'll be happy for me. I know the marriage is only temporary, and once it's over, we can go about our lives. I'll go back to helping you take care of Nathan. Maybe I'll even find a job in town. But everything will go back to normal. And he'll go back to doing what he does."

I had watched Julia for many years date so many guys. She never stayed with them very long, but she seemed happy. That was what this was: my chance to be carefree like her and to learn what that was like. But for some reason, she hated that idea.

Her lips thinned, and she shook her head. "You're right, Jami. I'm sorry. If you are happy, then so am I. Hamish isn't a bad guy, and I get why he wants that inheritance." She took a few steps forward until she was in front of me. "I'd love to come to your wedding. And if you'll still have me, I'd be honored to be your maid of honor."

I smiled. "Yes, you can. And as maid of honor, you have to help me find a dress. Since he is in hiding, the wedding isn't going to be in a church. It will take place in his suite, but that doesn't mean I don't need a dress."

Julia bit her lip. "I have the perfect dress for you—"

I held up my hands. "I don't want to wear your clothes. They look great on you, but they're not comfortable for me."

She chuckled. "They aren't meant to be comfortable. You're not going to get married in sweatpants, Jami."

"I know." Though, the thought of marrying in sweatpants was appealing. "I just want something of my own. A dress I picked out."

She studied me for a moment before nodding. "Right. I know The Blue Spot has a gift shop—"

"A gift shop? I can't get married in a T-shirt that says 'Castle Ridge: Neither A Castle, Nor A Ridge.'"

My sister laughed. "No, silly. It's an exclusive resort, so they have exclusive clothing there. Laura took me a few weeks ago. They have some really swanky things."

I was wary that a hotel gift shop was a good place to buy a wedding dress, but time was limited. As long as it was comfortable and easily removable for the wedding night, I'd wear it.

The wedding was only so Hamish could get his inheritance, but I looked at it as the perfect opportunity to lose my virginity. Being a virgin never really bothered me before, but now that I met Hamish, I desperately wanted to kick my virgin status to the curb.

"If you think they'd have something nice, we can check it out."

Julia went back to grab Nathan's basket before we headed inside. I waited for her to pack up his diaper bag so we could head on over to The Blue Spot to get me a dress.

Maybe I'd get a chance to slip away from Julia while we were there so I could go meet up with Hamish and try another practice kiss.

Chapter Fifteen

HAMISH

I managed to pull the toothbrush out of my mouth before I choked on it. After I spit, I looked up at the person standing behind me in the mirror and asked, "Don't you knock?"

Jenner leaned against the bathroom doorframe. "You said I should use my key."

He tugged at his tan suit jacket and slid his hand through his hair while he watched himself in the mirror. I stood there and folded my arms over my chest, thankful I at least had a towel wrapped around my hips before he opened the bathroom door.

"Thankfully I wasn't using the toilet." I rolled my eyes.

"That's why you lock the bathroom door when you have to go number one or number two."

I turned and leaned back against the white marble counter. "I don't know what to address first. The fact that this is my room, and I was alone, so why would I lock my door? Or the fact that you call it *number one* and *number two*."

"I have three younger siblings. I grew up in a house where the bathroom was called the potty, and what you did in the potty was number one and number two."

I rolled my lips over my teeth, trying to hold back the laughter. "So, then what's number three?"

He raised his eyebrow at me. "You don't want to know what number three is."

"Enough potty talk. Why are you here, other than to bask in my handsomeness?"

He opened his mouth, but right as he was about to say something, there was a knock at the door.

I went to move, but Jenner held up his hand. "We don't know who that is. It could be Dick or one of his spies. You wait here while I check it out."

"Before you go, have you found out anything about the murder charge?"

His lips thinned. That wasn't good.

"We'll discuss it after I answer the door. Basically, someone says they saw you leave the crime scene, and you had blood on your clothes."

Ugh. I leaned back on the counter, gripping it tight. That wasn't good, either.

Who could have seen me? I never met the victim, so how could anyone have seen me there? The more I found out, the more questions I had.

Jenner closed the bathroom door. I was shut in to steep in my own paranoia. Maybe I had met the victim. Was it some lonely worker at my company who I had met once but never remembered his name? Jenner tried to get information on Tiberius Endicott, but the only person he found was an old man, who was alive and well, living in a small town in Massachusetts.

It was odd that I was accused of killing a guy who never existed.

I was quickly knocked out of my thoughts by Jenner yelling, "Hey, you can't go in there."

Shit. It had to be Dick. How did he find me?

I thought about hiding in the shower, but that was pointless. There was a large pane of clear glass separating the shower from the rest of the bathroom, not exactly the best place to hide.

I sucked it up and decided to just accept that I had been beaten. I stood there with my arms crossed, ready to handle what was behind that door.

When it flung open, I said, "What are you... Jami?" My arms fell to my sides.

Jami was silent. Her infectious smile slowly slid from her face as her eyes drifted down my body, lingering on my abs. "You have no shirt on."

The corner of my lips crept up. "That's what happens when I've taken a shower."

"You have no shirt on."

"You've already mentioned that." I stepped forward and guided her farther into the bathroom. Behind her, I saw Jenner move toward us, so I quickly closed the door.

Jami cleared her throat. "I didn't expect you to be so..." Her words faded as she reached up toward my chest, then her hand stopped. "I shouldn't have come over. I mean, I should have texted you first. Prepared you." Her hand hung in the air between us.

I placed my hand behind hers and pulled it to my chest. "We're going to be married soon. You can touch me anytime you want."

Her fingers trembled as she touched me.

"Touch whatever you like."

"Okay," Jami said, but she hadn't moved.

"Let me help you."

But instead of moving her hand around my chest, I cupped her chin and pulled her in for a kiss. She was nervous, and I knew for absolute certainty that my lips were the cure for her anxiety.

A high-pitched sound came from the back of her throat before it lowered into a moan. That was all I needed to know that I had made the right decision.

My hands slid around until they tangled in her hair. She wore it down, free of her usual braid. My lips slid from her, over her chin and down her neck.

"Hamish," she groaned, and her voice sent a vibration down my spine, all the way down to my cock.

"God, Jami, why are you so soft?" I nipped at the apex of her neck.

"Laura gave me some lotion for Christmas."

My kissing stopped, and I raised my head. "What?"

With a lust-filled gaze, she said, "You asked why I had such soft skin. It's the lotion. It's called Mountain Berry —"

"No." I put my finger over her mouth. "That's not important. It was a question that needed no answer."

"Oh. Okay." A cute wrinkle appeared between her eyes.

Her hand, which hadn't moved an inch on my chest, slowly drifted down. Sparks of heat left a trail wherever her fingers meandered.

"Careful. You might cause my towel to fall." I doubted the towel would go too far, as my cock was now rock-hard and pinned against her stomach.

Her hand snapped back, and I regretted opening my mouth. "Sorry," she mumbled, her gaze drifting to the floor.

Shit.

I was only joking about the towel falling to the ground, but she didn't realize that. Taking a deep breath, I wondered how to rectify the situation. I never had to work this hard to be intimate with a woman before.

She must have sensed my uncertainty because Jami took a step back. I reached for my towel as it had actually loosened.

"We need to wait. I shouldn't have come in here."

She was right. Logically, we had to wait until we were legally married. But ever since our kiss yesterday, I hadn't stopped thinking about how she would feel when I got the chance to sink my cock deep inside her.

Would she whimper? Would her gorgeous chocolate eyes widen as I filled her? Or would she arch her back, trying to get my cock to sink deeper?

As I watched her reach for the door, I said, "Fuck it."

Grabbing her wrist, I pulled her back. The moment her body hit mine, my towel fell.

It wasn't a joke anymore.

My mouth crashed onto hers, and the second she opened to let me sink inside, I knew there was no going back. I reached around and cupped her ass, squeezing it.

She must have liked that because her leg tried to wrap around mine, but she was so short, she kept slipping. I reached down and lifted her. She wrapped her legs around me as I dug my fingers into her ass. I wanted to touch more of her body, so I turned and set her on the bathroom counter.

She held on to my shoulders tightly. I hoped she'd explore me a little more. Maybe if my fingers went on an expedition of her body, she'd do the same.

I reached up and cupped her tit. She made the slightest noise, and I almost didn't catch it. Her pale pink sweater was thin enough that I saw her perfect nipples harden, and my thumb drifted over one.

Jami pulled away from the kiss, her eyes wide.

"You didn't like that?" I asked.

"I don't know. It was… different. I felt it, but it just, uh…"

I knew she was a virgin, but she must have done some fooling around. Had she had an orgasm before?

"What exactly have you done with a guy before, Jami?"

I thought she might hesitate answering me as it was a personal question, but she quickly responded.

"Kissing. And I have seen and touched a penis before. My ex in college liked it when I pulled on his."

"I don't care what you did for him. What about you? What did he do for you?"

She appeared confused by the question and took a moment to answer. "Uh, he kissed me. Though he wasn't very good at it."

I pointed between her legs. "Down there. He kissed you down there?"

Her eyes widened. "No. Oh, no. I have read about that but never experienced it."

"You *read* about it?" I mumbled.

How sheltered had this woman been? I figured with a sister like Julia, she'd be aware of a lot more. And the more I thought about it, the angrier I became.

Not at Jami—I was angry with the people who cared for her. At the shitty ex who only seemed to care about making himself happy. At the sisters who should have told her what to expect from a man instead of reading about it in a book.

"Did you learn about the birds and the bees? You know, the sex talk?"

"Yes. I learned that when I was ten."

I let out a breath. That was a relief. Based on how she was reacting to me and what we had done, I worried I'd have to sit her down and give her the talk.

"Have you ever orgasmed before?"

She rolled her eyes. "Of course I have. Lots of times. Julia gave me a vibrator for my eighteenth birthday. She told me what it was for, and when I tried it, I realized it was the best gift I had ever received... other than Nancy."

Maybe Julia had educated her on men and sex after all.

I smiled. "Good, so she also told you what to expect from me and other men when it comes to sex?"

She tilted her head. "She told me about the guys she dated, but never really told me what to do when it comes to sex."

"How about Laura or your mom?"

She shook her head.

I sighed. Did they think she'd stay a virgin forever?

"Is this a problem?" she asked with worry etching her brow.

I reached up and removed her glasses, brushing away the golden strands that fell on her face. "No. It just means that we're going to have to try lots of different things to find out what you enjoy. Like when I rubbed your nipple." I lifted the front of her sweater until her bra was showing. She had on a white lace bra, and I itched to peel it back.

I lifted my gaze to hers to check if she was alright with what I had done.

"Okay?" I asked.

"Yes." Her response was quick but breathy.

"I'm going to peel back your bra cup."

Jami nibbled her bottom lip and nodded.

I slipped my finger under the lace, skimming her nipple. She sucked in a breath, but I kept going, tugging the lace back until her tit spilled out. The woman was petite, but not when it came to her chest.

My thumb lifted to my mouth and I sucked on it for a second. She watched in fascination as I lowered it back to her nipple. Circling it, Jami sucked in her lips.

"Does that feel good?" I asked.

My cock almost hurt it was so hard, but I held back from touching it. What I was doing now was all about pleasuring Jami. There was no way I'd be selfish like her ex. Once our marriage was over in two months, I wanted her to walk away with a huge smile on her face. A smile that told the world she was one satisfied woman.

I licked my other thumb and pushed back the other bra cup, doing the same to both tits. Jami's mouth fell open, but no sound emerged.

She was incredibly expressive, and her enjoyment was written all over her face.

"God, you're beautiful," I mumbled. I wanted to rip those jeans off her and sink deep inside.

When I clasped her nipples between my thumb and forefinger, giving her a slight pinch, her head fell back, and a guttural moan came out of her mouth.

My cock was dripping.

"Are you wet?"

"What?"

My hand slid from her breast until it settled between her legs. I pushed my hand against her apex and began to rub.

"Are you wet?" I asked again.

Her nose flared. "Yes."

"Good. Now take off your jeans."

She didn't hesitate. Jami unbuttoned her jeans, and I helped her slide them off so she could stay on the counter.

She sat there in nothing but her white lace panties with her tits hanging out and her sweater hitched up. Fuck, she was gorgeous.

I reached over and slid my finger up her thigh. "Spread your legs."

Jami shifted, but her legs weren't that far apart.

"Like this." I helped her, placing her feet up on the counter, spreading her as wide as she could go. "Now when I say spread your legs, you'll know what I mean."

She leaned back on her elbows. The woman was a dream. Whatever I had fantasized about her the past few days, it was nothing compared to what was happening right now.

With one hand I reached up, resuming my play with her nipple. The other hand slid up her thigh, goose flesh marking my path. When I got to the edge of her lace panties, I slid a finger inside.

Her back arched as my finger slipped over her folds. I studied her reaction to my touch. When my finger slipped inside her apex, and I rubbed her clit with my thumb, Jami's body began to vibrate.

"Hamish," she moaned.

I leaned over and gave her other nipple some attention with my tongue. Jami curled her fingers into my hair. I knew she wouldn't last very long, but I wanted to taste her as she came.

When I stood and dropped my hands, the look of disappointment in her eyes almost made me resume playing with her body.

"Is it over?" she asked.

I hooked my thumbs in her panties at her hips and pulled. She understood what I was doing and shifted to let me tug them away.

"Oh, I haven't even begun." I lowered to my knees and dropped her undies on the floor.

When I leaned in between her thighs, my nose flared at her scent—she smelled delicious. The moment I extended my tongue and had my very first taste, Jami jolted.

"Mmm," I hummed and wrapped my arm around her thigh to hold her in place. "Now you'll understand what I meant when I asked if your ex kissed you down here." I leaned in and gave her that kiss.

"Oh, Hamish," she said rather loudly as she reached for my head.

I kept lapping her up as her fingers tugged at my hair. And when I placed two fingers inside her, her hips started to shift.

I glanced up to find Jami staring at what I was doing. Her mouth sagged open, her lips glistening as she leaned back on one elbow. She kept jerking her hips, and I suspected she might be unsure how to handle what I was doing to her sweet pussy.

Lifting my head, her juices dripping down my chin, I said, "You can ride my face if you'd like. Grind into me. This is all about pleasuring you. I want to know what you like."

Jami completely understood what I said because once I got back to work licking her up, her hips shifted in a circular motion.

Her hand left my head, and I glanced up to see why. She was twisting and tugging her nipple. Her eyes glazed over, and her mouth sagged. She looked like the perfect wet dream.

"This feels so good. I love it when you suck my clit. Please, make me come," Jami said as her hips moved even faster.

I did as she commanded. My lips wrapped around her clit, and I sucked.

"Oh god, yes."

I watched as Jami shifted so she could grab both her spiked nipples and pinch them. She let out a deep groan, and I felt her tighten around my finger. I relished every second of that beautiful woman as she ricocheted over the edge.

Her head fell back as my name fell from her lips. I had never seen a woman as captivating as Jami was as she orgasmed.

My kisses eased and turned into soft licks. I was about to stand, scoop her up, and take her out to the bedroom when a knock on the door jolted me.

"Hamish." Jenner's voice came from the other side.

Jami jumped off the counter and scrambled for her clothes.

I quickly reached down and grabbed my towel. "Jenner? You're still here? I thought you had left."

I thought it was obvious I wanted to be alone with my fiancée when I slammed the bathroom door in his face.

"I had left. But I just got a call from my assistant in New York. Somehow Dick found out you are here at The Blue Spot. He only suspected before, but I think Jami telling him she's your fiancée tipped him off, and he began paying off staff for information."

That fucking weasel.

"Anyway, we need to get you out of here. Also, Jami will marry you, and I have all the paperwork. I suggest we head over to the minister's house and do a quick ceremony. That way, even if you get arrested, you'll be married. There's nothing Dick can do about that."

Jami stopped what she was doing, her arm only through one sweater hole. "Today?" she asked.

I secured the towel around my torso again. "Is that okay? I know it's short notice, but—"

Her arms embraced me, and she let out an excited yelp. "Yes! Then we can go on our honeymoon." She leaned back and gave me an exaggerated wink.

A chuckle escaped my throat. She was adorable.

"Okay, Jenner. Contact Rock and Jami's sisters. Tell them we are about to get hitched." I smiled and then leaned down to kiss my future wife on her forehead.

Chapter Sixteen

JAMI

My face began to hurt. I was unaware grinning could cause pain. I guess I never smiled enough to discover that. But I didn't care about the pain. This was the happiest moment of my life.

I was getting married.

My fingers were wrapped around a bunch of plastic daisies. They had dust on them, and every time I moved them, I ended up sneezing. Even if my flowers were fake, my simple white slip dress was lovely.

When Julia took me shopping at The Blue Spot's gift shop, The Blue Bag, I wasn't paying attention to what she showed me, saying *yes* to whatever dress looked the whitest. How could there be so many different shades of white?

Even when I tried it on to see if it fit, I didn't really look in the mirror. I wanted the shopping to be over so I could go see Hamish, and it was worth running off from my sister to visit him in his room. The way he touched me in his bathroom, I didn't know how the honeymoon could ever beat that.

"Do you take Hamish Theodore Maximilian Blackwell as your husband, to have and to hold—"

"Yes," I said, unable to wait for the minister to finish.

He lived in a small wooden cabin in the mountains. The place was sparse with just a few chairs and one small table in the kitchen area. My sisters, Rock, and Jenner all had to stand near the front door as there wasn't much room for them.

"Do you, Hamish, take Jami Lucy Nutters as your wife, to have and to—"

Hamish grinned down at me. "Yes."

I liked when he smiled. The way he looked at me now, even after just having an orgasm back at the resort, made my nipples harden.

He was incredibly handsome in the jeans, red flannel shirt, and suspenders Jenner picked out for him. Hamish had to sneak out of The Blue Spot unnoticed, so he wore a cap, but took it off for the ceremony. But for some reason, I never noticed before how sexy he was in that outfit.

My jaw tightened, and I glanced over at the minister. The guy had white whiskers and not much hair left on his head, and he wouldn't stop talking. Shouldn't the ceremony be over by now? Hamish and I needed to start our honeymoon.

"If there is anyone here who believes these two should not be married, let them speak now or forever hold their peace," the minister said.

I narrowed my eyes and stared at Julia. She had better not say a word. But my sister just stood there and smiled at me. I noticed a tear fall from her eye.

I cleared my throat, as more than enough time had passed for anyone to say something. The minister needed to wrap things up.

"Then, with the power invested in me by the Church of the Mountain People and Woodland Creatures, and the State of Virginia, I now pronounce you husband and wife. You may kiss the bride, but if you're going to do that, I suggest you two take it outside. I don't want sinners in this house."

Hamish narrowed his eyes. "How are we sinning if we just got married?"

The minister pointed at Hamish. "All kissing is the work of the devil."

"Come on, you two. Let's move the party outside," Jenner said, waving us toward the door.

Once we were out of the cabin and the minister locked the door behind us, I whirled around and threw my arms around Hamish. I kissed him before he could say a word. And I kept kissing him even after I heard several people clear their throats.

Heat burned inside me, and I wanted him more than I had in his bathroom. But Hamish pulled back. I worried he didn't desire me anymore. Now that he was married and could claim the inheritance, maybe he didn't feel the need to have sex with me.

It was all for the money, and he was using me.

When his gaze fell on me, I could have sworn I saw the same heat reflected back. But it wasn't real. Maybe Julia was right. He had experience in playing it cool and being with women.

I was so easily duped.

The tears burned the back of my eyes.

"What's wrong?" he whispered in my ear.

"I don't want to be here," I said, but what I really wanted was to scream, *You're a liar!*

He plucked the fake flowers from my hands. I had been so entranced by Hamish, I forgot I was holding them. Outstretching his arm, Jenner took them from him.

Then he reached down and picked me up, just like he had in the bathroom. Only this time, he didn't place me on a counter; this time he walked toward a large black car.

There was a man standing there who opened the door when Hamish and I came near. He wore a black suit and stared straight ahead as if we weren't right in front of him.

Hamish bent but lost his footing. I tumbled half in and half out of the car.

"Sorry. It was harder than I expected to carry you into the car. Sort of an awkward angle."

"You didn't have to do that. I can get in the car myself." I pushed myself up and moved into my seat.

Once he was inside, the door closed behind him. "I know, but it's the tradition of carrying the bride over the threshold." He shrugged. "I wanted something traditional since this was the craziest slapped-together wedding I have ever encountered."

I blinked. That was kind of sweet.

"You do care," I said as I reached for his hand.

"Yes." He gave a soft smile. "You are my wife. I know we're only married so I can get my inheritance, but I really want to make you happy, Jami. I like you."

My cheeks warmed. "I like you too."

The car began to move, and I hadn't a clue where the driver was taking us. I never said goodbye to my sisters or Rock. And as unusual as that was, I was still blissfully happy, content to be seated next to a sweet man who cared about me.

"I'm not one of those men who wondered who I might end up marrying... I thought I'd never marry. But right now, I feel like the luckiest guy in the world." He reached up and pushed my hair off my shoulder, letting his thumb rub the neglected spot. "You made the most bewitching bride I've ever laid eyes on. All I wanted was that minister to call us husband and wife so I could take you home and peel the dress off."

I shifted closer until the seatbelt was digging into my hip. He reached out and scooped up my hand, lifting it to his lips. My body burned wherever his lips touched. I never thought kissing the back of a wrist could be so sexy. My core ached for him.

"That's why I kept cutting him off. I knew what he was going to say. I felt like we could skip that part and get on with the 'I do's.'"

He laughed, and it vibrated up my arm all the way to my heart.

"I noticed," he said in between dotting my arm with little kisses.

The car began to swerve, and I fell forward, my chest hitting his. When I looked up, his eyes smoldered.

"Where are we going?" I asked, unable to hold out much longer.

Would it be rude to make out with my husband in a car while a stranger was driving?

"My grandfather had a small home here in the mountains. I feared Dick might know about it, but Jenner asked around, and Dick had never been to it. I suspected Grandfather never told him about it."

"As long as it has a bedroom, I'll be happy." I winked again. I had finally figured out the wink. It made Hamish smile, so I guessed I was doing it right.

"Don't have to worry about that." He turned to look out the window. "In fact, we're coming up on it. You can judge for yourself, but just remember, it is small."

I leaned past Hamish and noticed a wooden home that looked like one of those Swiss chalets, but not very big. It appeared to be about the size of my home. I guessed, to a billionaire like Hamish, our house was small.

"Oh, I like it. I'm used to a home that size."

I leaned back, and his brow wrinkled. Glancing out the window again, he shook his head.

"Not the servants' quarters. I'm talking about the one next to it, a little farther back from the road."

I leaned over him again and gasped.

What he considered small was larger than the biggest building in Castle Ridge, which was the town government building. It housed the courts, the mayor's office, and the park services.

The car swerved and came to a stop. Hamish waited for the driver to run around the car and open the door.

Once he did, Hamish got out and immediately reached down to help me exit the car. My mouth hung open as I stared up at a four-story home. It looked like the servants' quarters, but about ten times larger. And behind it stood mountains filled with autumn-colored trees.

"I believe this will make a good temporary home. What do you think, Jami?"

Hamish waited for me to answer, and I could tell he was worried I wouldn't be happy. But what he didn't realize was I had lost the ability to speak.

In one day, I had the best orgasm of my life by a gorgeous billionaire. Not only that, but I became his wife, and now we got to live in what I could only describe as a mountain fairytale estate.

I used the only word that came to me. The only thing my mouth could form: "Yes."

Chapter Seventeen

HAMISH

"Let's try this again," I said as I held out my arms.

My beautiful bride's brow furrowed. "Try what again?"

"Carrying you over the threshold."

It was rather embarrassing what happened when I tried to place Jami in the car, so I wanted to show her I could do it. I felt the urge to prove to her I was a strong, capable husband.

Not that I needed to prove anything since the marriage was only temporary. Yet, for Jami, everything felt real. It was important that I do it right.

"Okay." She bent her knees, and I scooped her up. She had discarded her cream leather ankle boots by the front door of the house, so her bare feet kicked the air in my arms.

She was in awe of my grandfather's chalet when I walked her through the main floor. She exclaimed that Laura would love the rustic-designed kitchen.

Upon opening the door to the master bedroom, Jami gasped. "Wow. It's so beautiful."

Not as stunning as you.

Her silky white dress hugged her breasts, and it was difficult to keep my eyes off her chest, which meant I almost toppled her as I ran into the gray, wooden four-poster bed. She rolled onto the quilted bedspread, and I fell face-first next to her.

"Totally meant to do that," I mumbled with a chuckle as I crawled up beside her.

She was gazing up at the large skylight as the late afternoon sun filtered in. "I never knew this was here. Living in Castle Ridge my whole life, I thought I had seen everything in and around the town. I guess I was wrong."

I shrugged as I reached up to her dress strap on her shoulder, tugging it down. "Since it's made of wood, it blends into the scenery from afar. And my grandfather's property extends for a while. I doubt you could ever get close enough to see it."

Leaning in, I kissed her shoulder. Her skin was soft, and I never wanted to take my lips off it.

"Since we married and you honored your grandfather's wishes, does that mean you now own this place?"

"Yes," I said, but I didn't really want to talk about it anymore.

We were alone, married, and in a bed. There was no reason to do anything else but explore each other's bodies. I felt the best part of the day was almost here—her gifting me with her virginity.

I hesitated as that thought entered my head. What if that was why she kept talking? Maybe she didn't want to lose her virginity.

It wasn't as if we had to have sex in order to fulfill my grandfather's request. We didn't even need to see each other again if she wanted that. I wanted to see her every day, but what if the marriage meant something different for her?

I felt like an asshole.

Sitting back, I watched Jami. She was gazing toward the large sliding glass door that led out to the stone deck with a view of the mountains and gardens in the backyard.

"I know this is our honeymoon, but we don't need to have sex if you don't want to. Just because we are married, I don't want you to feel obligated to have sex with me."

She turned to face me. "I know, but I want to have sex with you. I want you to be the man who teaches me. You're gentle and patient, which I need." Jami bit her lip, and her eyes cast down as she fiddled with her fingers.

My cock pushed against my jeans. It wanted out from the stiff fabric, to find a warm, soft home between Jami's legs.

"I don't know how patient I'll be, but I can promise to try," I said as I unbuttoned my flannel shirt, peeling it off me.

She studied me as I undressed.

"I haven't seen you naked before... only your chest. When we were in the bathroom, I didn't get a good look at you when your towel fell because I was too busy finding my clothes," she commented as I unfastened my jeans and awkwardly removed them, along with my black boxer briefs.

"Do you want to explore my body the way I did to you in the bathroom?" I asked. The way she was looking at me,

I thought she was about to take a bite out of my thigh.

She nodded and reached over, grabbing my hard cock rather firmly. I was surprised that she went right for it. I thought she might take her time and feel more of the rest of my body first.

Jami rolled her hand up and down my shaft. My eyes shut because it felt incredible, and when I opened them again, I noticed she just sat there with a bored expression.

I placed my hand over hers to stop her. "I want you to explore my body because you want to, not to just get me off. I'm your husband; have fun." I slid my hand up her arm, tugging the other dress strap down enough that her tits fell out.

I cupped her breast and made sure to pinch her nipple before I let go. Jami inhaled deeply. She reached for the hem of her dress and pulled it effortlessly over her head. She sat there in just her white lace panties—the same ones I dropped on my bathroom floor just hours earlier.

"I can't get over how gorgeous you are." I leaned back on my elbow and rested my head on my hand. I moved my hands to her body, skimming my fingers over her stomach and hips.

She reached out for me, mirroring what I was doing to her. Once she got near my cock, she stopped. "Can I taste you?"

"Of course we can kiss." I leaned forward, but she shook her head.

"I don't mean that. Not that I don't like kissing you. I enjoy that a lot. But I meant your penis. Can I do to you what you did to me earlier?"

My nostrils flared. "You want to suck my cock?"

"Yes. But I've never done it before, so you will have to tell me what you like."

I tried to speak, but nothing came out, so I nodded. Reaching over, I plucked her glasses from her face, hoping she wasn't too blind without them. Once I placed the glasses safely on the wrought iron table next to the bed, I lay back against the white linen pillow.

"You can start by kissing it. Nothing intense, just soft kisses. And licks. Like you would do to a lollipop or an ice cream cone."

It wasn't easy giving her instructions. Once I started to list comparable examples, an image of her lips on those things popped into my head. My heart was pounding, and she hadn't even lowered her head to my cock yet.

Jami bent over, her hair falling all around her. I helped her gather it up and held my breath as her lips pressed against my rigid cock.

My fist tightened around her hair as she began to explore my cock, licking up the pre-come. Once she had done that a few times, I instructed her to wrap her hand around the base and tug it up and down while she licked and sucked.

If I hadn't known her, I would have never guessed this was her first time. Jami instantly understood what I liked. I was surprised when she swirled her tongue around my tip as I never told her to do that.

The sight of Jami's plump lips sucking my cock was going to send me over the edge. I knew I wouldn't last if she kept it up.

I cupped her cheek, and she glanced up, her lips making a popping sound as she removed my cock from her mouth.

"Is there anything wrong?"

I shook my head. "No. In fact, it's too good. I would end up coming if you kept it up."

"Okay."

"I want to be inside you when that happens." I waved her up to me, and my lips crashed onto hers. I plunged inside her the moment her mouth opened.

We hadn't kissed long before I rolled her onto her back. Moving down her neck, I found her nipple and sucked one into my mouth. I loved how she squirmed at my touch.

I didn't last long on her tit as I kept moving down. My mouth watered for another taste of her sweet pussy.

"Spread your legs."

I sat back and admired how she learned to do exactly what I asked. I wanted to take my time, but my balls would hate me if I did that. So, I lowered myself and licked her glistening folds.

Jami was louder this time. Before she barely made any noise, but now her moans and groans were constant. And once I placed my fingers inside her, she came.

I guess she was about to go over the edge too.

Reaching over to the nightstand, I opened the black lacquered wooden box. Grabbing a condom, I ripped it open and rolled it on my cock in record time. I had made sure there were plenty of condoms here before I took my bride home.

Jami was watching me, and I realized she had never seen a man put on a condom before.

"Keep your legs open."

She pulled her legs farther apart, and I placed my cock at the apex of her thighs. Jami was hot as I slowly pushed inside.

I looked up when she squealed. "I'm taking this slow. It will hurt for a few seconds since it's your first time, but it should fade after that. If at any point you want me to stop, just tell me."

I could tell she was holding her breath, but she nodded. I paused every few seconds as I pushed farther inside. All I wanted to do was slam into her and fuck her until she begged to come.

That was what I normally did with women, but Jami was different. It wasn't that she required a lighter touch; I just wanted to be softer with her. I wanted to caress her more, kiss her more, and do whatever was needed to please her.

Her nipples were spikes, so I leaned over and sucked one into my mouth. Jami moaned out a "yes" as I lapped at her tit.

I went to suck her other nipple in my mouth and as I did, I made my final push inside her.

"Oh, Hamish."

I glanced up, worried she was in pain. But I didn't need to worry as she arched her back in bliss. I shifted and eased out and back in once again. Pretty soon I was rocking back and forth as her nails dug into my hips.

I lifted onto my arms, and both Jami and I watched my cock fill her. Her tits bounced as I began to pick up my pace and pounded into her pussy.

"God, you're so wet."

I wanted to reach between her legs but not like this. I took my hand off her breast and leaned back on my haunches, placing my thumb on her clit.

"Hamish, yeah, make me come."

Jami was so slippery as I worked her. She pinched her nipples, and I knew she wasn't going to last long. I loved how she did what she liked. She discovered nipple play turned her on, so she had no trouble doing that in front of me.

I expected shyness with her about sex, but it was the opposite. The woman tried whatever I suggested.

"I'm coming," she said as I felt her pussy tighten.

My eyes fell to where I was fucking her and watched as she dripped down my cock and thighs. I slathered her cum over the base of my cock.

Her hand reached down from her breast.

"Oh god, don't stop." Her fingers slid over her clit.

I slipped out of her in an instant. Before she could ask what was happening, I grabbed her hips and helped flip her around so she was on her hands and knees. Then I slid back inside her, and her glazed eyes stared back at me in satisfaction.

"We should try all the positions during our honeymoon."

Her pussy was dripping all over my cock. Jami reached back and resumed playing with her clit.

Her head flipped back as she let out a loud groan. I knew it wouldn't be long for her.

I couldn't hold out any longer. My balls tightened, and I cried out, "I'm coming."

I didn't know if Jami heard me as I felt her come again on my cock.

My balls tingled as the last of my cum spilled into her. I fell forward and cradled Jami in my arms as we lay down on our sides.

We both were sweaty and breathing heavily, but I couldn't let go. What she just shared with me was the most amazing thing anyone had ever done.

Sure, I had sex before, but that was all it was. Just sex. Fucking. This was more than that. Deeper.

I had known Jami for less than a week, and I wondered if I was falling in love with her.

Chapter Eighteen

JAMI

I tried to hold back a giggle as I slipped into the kitchen. Tiptoeing up behind Hamish, I lifted my arms ready to surprise him.

But he must've heard me because he jumped around, spatula in hand, and wrapped me in his arms.

I gasped as he nuzzled his face into my neck. We had been married for three days, and I was blissfully happy. If I had known that marriage would make me joyous, I would have hunted down a husband long ago.

Maybe it was just Hamish who kept me content?

"What are you doing?" I asked as I slid from his arms.

"Making pancakes."

I glanced around him to the pan that sat on a six-burner stovetop. Everything in the kitchen was made to look rustic or antique, but I was pretty sure ovens weren't as big as a small car a hundred years ago.

I frowned. "What sort of pancakes?"

"Blueberry." Hamish grinned.

He appeared so radiant that it hurt me when I said, "They don't look like any blueberry pancakes I've ever seen."

"Uh…" He glanced back around and flipped the pancake over, which only confused me more.

"For one thing, they're pink. And what are those black things? Did you put chocolate chips in it?"

If I had to guess what they were without him telling me, I would have said hash browns made from sweet potatoes.

"Aren't blueberries pink?"

I took a step back. "No, not ever. It has the word blue in the name. They are *blue*… berries."

"Then what did I use?" He walked over to the large refrigerator that was made to look like a regular wooden cabinet. Once he opened the door, he pulled out a glass container with something purple inside.

"I used this."

He handed it over and I had no idea what was in the container. Once I opened it, the scent caused my eyes to widen.

"These aren't blueberries or any type of berry. It's not even fruit. You used chopped purple cabbage in your pancakes."

He frowned and walked over to the pancake, removing it from the pan and placing it on a plate beside the stove. "Maybe they don't taste bad."

"You tried my cranberry sauce, so I'll try your pancakes." I reached up to his cheek and gave him a kiss.

It was our third morning as a married couple, and I wanted to be supportive. He was patient with me when he taught me the different ways we could have sex. I was unaware of all the positions that could be achieved with sex.

Hamish deserved a wife who stood by his side and showed how much she cared for him.

Not waiting for a fork, I pulled off a piece of the pancake. He watched me as I tucked it into my mouth.

It was crunchy. I chewed a bit more, and that was when the cabbage flavor hit me. I liked cabbage, even with a little sweetness, like with coleslaw, but this wasn't coleslaw.

I make my way over to the large farmhouse sink and spit it out of my mouth. "It's disgusting."

"It can't be that bad," he said right before popping a piece between his lips.

He had about three chews before he joined me at the sink.

"You're right. Ugh, I wanted to make you a nice honeymoon breakfast instead of Daniel making it for us, for once."

I slid my arms around his waist. Hamish was so tall that my head barely touched his chest. I had left my glasses upstairs by the bed, but even a little blurry, he was still devastatingly handsome.

"We can order food or call Laura and ask her if we can come over for breakfast."

He shook his head. "I'll just have Daniel do it."

Stepping back, I nodded.

The cook. He used to be Hamish's grandfather's chef but had been on leave since his grandfather's death. Jenner asked him a few days ago if he'd be willing to come back to cook, and he agreed.

I had heard stories through my sister about personal chefs, and they were always terrible tales. It was always where the person who hired the chef was awful and demanded outrageous things.

Ever since Hamish told me that we had a personal cook, I worried Daniel would think what I requested would be too difficult. I didn't want him telling tales about me.

"Okay, but we really shouldn't bother him too much. I'll be happy with whatever he feels like making."

Hamish threw his head back and laughed. He guided me over to the round kitchen table, and we sat. The kitchen had brown wood cabinets with white walls, but the kitchen table was a large round marble table, complete with upholstered chairs with brown, gray and white stripes. Everything was luxurious in the home, even when it wasn't made to appear decadent.

"Jami, I pay Daniel a good salary. His job is to cook what I like, not what he likes."

"I know, but—"

Hamish reached for my hands, pulling them into his lap. "Jami, don't worry what other people think. It doesn't matter. I know you aren't used to people waiting on you, but I am. I have the means to pay them for their service."

That sounded cold, but still, I didn't like it. "Just because you have money doesn't mean you can treat them however you want."

"No, it doesn't." He rubbed his thumb over the back of my hand, and my shoulders sagged. "But just because you have people who work for you doesn't mean you should let them take advantage of you, either. If you pay someone, they should do what is needed."

The back of my eyes began to burn. It made sense what he was saying, but it wasn't what I wanted.

"I don't want people to do things for me. I can do these things myself. And if I don't know how to do it, I'll learn. I went to university; I can learn." A tear rolled down my face.

"Whoa." Hamish scooted his chair closer to me, placing his arm around my shoulder. "I don't think we're talking about servants anymore, are we?"

I wiped away my tear and shook my head. "My whole life everyone thought I was stupid or weak, or that I would always have to rely on other people to take care of me. And for the longest time... I believed them."

I frowned and turned to him, burying my face in his chest. The tears flowed freely; there was no holding them back. Hamish put his other arm around me, holding me tight.

"But once Julia had Nathan, I started to doubt them. Here was this little baby who really did need people to take care of him, and who did my sister trust the most with her son? *Me.* I was the one who set up his feeding routine. I was the one who made sure he made his appointments and was changed regularly. I love my sister, but she doesn't understand the power of a routine. It was up to me to enforce it. If I could take care of that little baby, then I knew I could take care of myself."

"I know you can. It never entered my mind that anyone would think of you as anything but strong and smart and the sweetest person to ever walk the planet."

I shook my head. "It's just... you haven't known me very long."

And that was what worried me. What would happen when I messed up? When I did to him what I did to Nathan when I got arrested? Laura was angry at me for ruining her car. How angry would Hamish get when I screwed up something important to him?

He softly kissed my head. "I don't need to know the old Jami. The past is the past. I am sure if you met me five or ten years ago, you'd think I was a jerk. But we grow and change and learn. In fact, we'll learn together."

I eased back and glanced up at him, blinking away my tears. "Learn together? Like with sex?"

He smirked. "That too. But I was thinking more like a skill. Perhaps we could help each other learn how to cook. We both don't know how, so let's learn together."

"Really? You want to learn how to cook?"

He nodded. "In the meantime, we have Daniel cook for us. But we teach ourselves so that one day we can make a few meals instead of him."

Nobody ever wanted to do what I liked. My sisters always had their own thing, so I got used to doing things alone.

"That would be fun."

Maybe there was more to marriage than just sex.

Chapter Nineteen

HAMISH

"I hope I'm not interrupting." Jenner walked into the kitchen.

"Of course not. Want to join in?" I pulled Jami in for a hug.

Jenner held up his hands. "This is a new suit. I'll hang out in the doorway for fear it might get ruined."

"Have it your way." I smiled and raised my flour-covered finger, moving closer to him.

It had been five days since the wedding, and Jami and I were having a blast. It was like living with my best friend, but we got to have sex any time we wanted. It was the best.

Jenner took a step away from me. "If you touch me, I will quit."

He had interrupted one of our cooking lessons—which wasn't so much a cooking lesson as just an excuse to get dirty so we could get naked and have sex. There was one cooking lesson we had where we didn't get dirty, but we kept feeding each other the food until we ended up having sex. All the lessons just ended in sex.

"Okay. I won't." I grinned at him, totally planning on swiping flour on his nose before he left.

"I swear it's as if you two decided marriage means you can act like children. What's this I heard about you two playing hide and seek?"

"How did you hear about that?" Jami asked.

Flour covered every part of her clothes and exposed skin, except for her right cheek.

"I keep tabs on you two and ask the servants how you're doing, just in case Dick finds you, or you're arrested again."

My eyes slid to Jami, and hers met mine.

I wasn't so concerned that Jenner was spying on us as I was about the hide and seek part.

"What exactly did they say about us playing hide and seek?"

"That you two were like kids, giggling and running around the house playing silly games."

"But nothing about what we did once we found each other hiding, right?"

Jenner tilted his head. "Why would they talk about that?"

"It's not important. Just… forget I brought it up." I waved it off as a cloud of flour filled the air.

Our game of hide and seek involved sex. Why? Because we were adults. Whoever found the hidden person got to dictate the sexual position. Jami seemed to always pick doggie style, while I preferred reverse cowgirl, though we sometimes switched it up.

"You both realize this is a temporary marriage? It's just for the inheritance," Jenner said.

"God, Jenner, we're just having some fun. Am I not allowed to do that? This is our house with our things."

He sighed and nodded. "You're right. I'm sorry. I guess I'm a little on edge because someone has arrived in town who makes me nervous. It's actually the reason I came over today."

I dusted off some of the flour on my clothes and sat on a barstool at the island counter. "Who?"

"Katherine Alejandro."

My mouth fell open, and I was glad I had sat down because I started feeling lightheaded.

"Who's Katherine Alejandro?" Jami asked, coming up behind me, rubbing my back.

Even her touch wouldn't help the dread that filled my chest.

"She's the New York State District Attorney. It's her office that wants to arrest Hamish for murder."

"But I've already been arrested. I'm out on bail." I shook my head totally confused.

"Yes, but there's new evidence, so new charges. I haven't got all the details yet, but I just want to warn you."

"And if she's here, then that means she thinks I'm here."

I raised my head and stared at Jenner. We both blurted out "Dick" at the same time.

"That jerk must have tipped off her office that I was here," I mumbled.

"I'm not sure about that. He is friends with Kodi Corradi, and I'm pretty sure Kodi turned on Dick to get a lighter sentence. I can't imagine Dick would walk into the DA's office just for a tip on your whereabouts. He hates you, but he loves himself more. I bet he had one of his buddies contact the DA about you."

"I thought there was no direct evidence linking what Kodi had done and Dick?" I asked.

"Not that the public knows. But I can't imagine the DA doesn't have something, no matter how small, on Dick. I think that's why he wants the inheritance. If he has enough money, then he can bribe corrupt judges and crooked law enforcement so he can get off. At the very least, if he was convicted, he'd get a shorter sentence. It's not just about beating you, Hamish... it's about saving his ass."

I threw my hands up. "Well, it's too late. I'm married. I got my wife right here to prove it." I slapped Jami on her tight ass, causing more flour to circle the air.

Jenner ran his hands through his hair. "If Dick is still in town now that the DA is in Castle Ridge, then he still thinks he has a chance at that money."

"Does he even know we're married?" Jami asked as her hand reached down for mine. "It's not like we made it public."

"Of course he does. That man has spies everywhere. And I made sure Rock let it slip that you married a very young woman recently. Gossip about Hamish spreads faster than Jack the Ripper through Whitechapel."

I blinked at my lawyer. He was stressed.

Rubbing my chin, I said, "If he knows I'm married, and the DA's in town, then maybe he's turned his sights on her."

"What do you mean?" Jenner asked.

"He knows he's beat. I married a twenty-one-year-old virgin. The paperwork has been signed and sent to the right people. He's smart enough to understand that he can't fight Granddad's will. Maybe he wants to find out what the DA has on me and, maybe, what the DA has on him too."

Jenner nodded. "That could be a possibility." He held up two fingers and crossed them. "We can hope. You two stay here. Unless the DA gets a warrant, she can't get to you. I'm going to reach out to my sources and find out what I can." Jenner's phone went off, and he held up his hand, walking into the dining room for privacy.

"I'm worried." Jami tugged at some strands of white-powdered hair.

I was concerned too, but I wasn't about to let her know. It was my job as her husband to protect her. It upset me that the best thing I could do was sit and do nothing. How could I protect my wife from the scrutiny I knew she'd receive just by being related to me? Or worse, from Dick, if I couldn't go anywhere.

I lifted our entwined hands and kissed one of her fingertips. "I know this isn't ideal, but I trust Jenner. And I can't be convicted of something I never did."

She rolled her eyes. "Maybe in your world, but here in places like Castle Ridge, bad things happen to good people all the time. As much as it was my fault for driving without a license, it didn't stop the cop from arresting me. No one, including the sheriff, thought I should have been arrested. Yet I got thrown in jail."

I leaned over and gave her a small peck on her lips. "So you admit that you're a good person."

She was more than a good person. Jami was the best person I had ever met. I'd trust her with my life and my fortune.

"I think so. But that incident taught me that I was human. Not that I thought I wasn't human, but my emotions clouded my judgment and put my nephew at risk. At the time, I thought the cop was right in arresting me. I was angry at myself for not seeing what was right in front of me. But you taught me that you can't always know what to do in every situation. Even if you study it, once you go through it, things happen that you can't predict."

I tilted my head. "I taught you that?"

Her cheeks turned pink through the flour. "Yes. Just because I was a virgin didn't mean I knew nothing. I spent a lot of time looking up sex and trying to learn what to do for when the time came. But when you kissed me, everything I learned evaporated. I had to experience your touch to understand my needs."

I was about to lean in and kiss her when Jenner came back into the kitchen. He held up the phone before placing it on the kitchen island counter.

"I just got off the phone with Rock. Looks like the DA is also staying at The Blue Spot. I'm going to head over there and see if I can find out anything. Maybe sit near her at dinner or in the Blue Bean. I might overhear something."

"I think she might recognize you. I still have the jeans and flannel you can borrow to go incognito," I said with a smile.

"No." Jenner was as much a suit snob as I was.

"And a baseball cap to cover up your hair," Jami said and walked to the front hallway.

When she came back, she held a dark blue hat.

"That's a trucker hat." Jenner plucked it from her fingers. "And it says, *I like it wet.*"

"I get trucker and baseball hats confused all the time. It doesn't matter. Most people in town wear one or the other."

Jenner's expression was one of repulsion as he eyed the hat. "No, thank you—"

"Jenner, if I had to go incognito, then so do you. I have hidden in a dilapidated room for several days, wore that hat to my wedding, and haven't been out in public in a week and a half. Now it's your turn."

"I'm not the one wanted for murder or trying to claim a large inheritance."

I stood and walked over to him, ignoring the fear in his eyes as I slapped my hand on his shoulder, effectively marking him with my flour power.

"No, but you're the lawyer of the guy who is wanted for murder and getting a large inheritance. I wonder how much you could charge the guy with the big inheritance for having to go incognito?"

I knew Jenner would consider it once I mentioned money.

"Done." He leaned away, causing my hand to drop.

He began to walk toward the front hallway before I called out, "You forgot this."

"No, I got the hat, Hamish—" He stopped himself when he looked back to notice I had his phone in my hand.

"Yes, that's important too." Jenner chuckled, grabbed it from me, and then waved goodbye.

He had lost more phones since I had known him than the years I had been alive. The man was great at just about anything he did, except keeping phones.

I just hoped he was better at discovering what the DA was here for than he was at holding on to phones.

Chapter Twenty

JAMI

I woke up to the smell of bacon. I guessed Laura didn't have to go into work until later today...

My eyes fluttered open, and I stared up at a skylight. Blinking, it took me a moment to remember that I wasn't at home anymore. I lived in a huge chalet on Hamish's estate.

You would have thought that after a week and a half of marriage I'd remember that by now, but every morning I woke up and thought I was back in my old bed.

Sitting up, I gazed around. The bed was about four times the size of the one I had at home.

"Good. You're awake." Hamish stood in the doorway in all his naked glory and held a wooden tray.

"Where's Daniel?"

"I gave him the day off. It's up to me to serve you today." Hamish smiled in a way that let me know he wasn't thinking about serving me food.

Our entire marriage had consisted of sex, sex, food, sex, sleep, cooking lessons—which just ended with sex—and then more sex. I never realized how much sex people had. And each time we fucked, it was better than the last.

No wonder Julia talked about it so much. It was amazing. Hamish made it spectacular and satisfied me every time. Whatever I asked for, he gave.

I felt comfortable around him, like I could tell him anything, and he'd never judge me. I hadn't felt that comfortable around a guy before, even most women, except for my family. I rarely opened up to people.

He placed the tray in the middle of the bed, but I shook my head. "It looks like a gorgeous day. Let's sit out on the deck and have breakfast."

I got up and shrugged on the plush gray robe that was here when we arrived. It was strange to discover a closet filled with clothes, all my size. I had never chosen an article of clothing that was in the wardrobe, but I guessed that was what it was like being a billionaire.

I opened the door and stepped onto the stone deck. The sun warmed my face as I inhaled the crisp autumn air, thankful it wasn't too cold yet.

I took the tray from Hamish as he went to put on his matching robe. Once he got outside, I placed the dishes on the round wooden table.

We were quiet for a few minutes, enjoying the bacon and Danishes while admiring the stunning view. It didn't matter how long I lived here, I would never stop loving the scenery.

I took a sip of coffee as Hamish said, "I think I should show you around the estate today."

"That sounds nice. Maybe later we can invite my sisters up here. I know Laura would love your kitchen."

He chuckled. "You keep saying my kitchen, but it's now *our* kitchen. This is your home, Jami. That's why I want to show you the estate. We both own the land."

I placed my coffee mug on the table. "You say that, but it's only true for the next few months. Didn't Jenner set the divorce date for January first? After that, this all goes back to you."

His jaw tightened. Had I said something wrong? Maybe I messed up the divorce date. It wasn't like I was happy all this had to end. But the marriage was never meant to last.

I loved my sisters and missed them, but with Hamish I felt like an adult. Not just because I was married. It was how he treated me. To him, I was his wife, not someone who needed help with everything.

Being here made me realize most people, including my sisters sometimes, spoke down to me like I was a child. Hamish never did that, not once.

We were both learning to cook together since we had been incredibly bad at it. Yes, we were flawed humans, just like everyone else in the world. But here, there was no one to judge us or tell us we couldn't do something.

It was paradise, and I never wanted it to end.

"Whatever you like," he mumbled.

I turned to him. "Is something wrong? You seem upset."

He was about to speak, but his phone buzzed from the bedroom. Groaning, Hamish got up and went back into the bedroom. I took the moment to enjoy another sip of coffee. He must have gotten his coffee from the Blue Bean. That stuff was addictive.

"That's weird," Hamish said as he came back to the table.

I looked over as he sat on the navy-blue padded chair. "What?"

"Jenner just texted me. He wants both of us to meet him back at the minister's home in two hours. I asked why, and he responded that the minister missed something during the ceremony. To make it legal, we basically have to do it again."

I thought back to what the minister did. Nothing about the ceremony was unusual, other than what Hamish was wearing.

"It seemed fine to me…"

"Right?" Hamish nodded. "Other than it was quick and in a cabin, there was nothing that wouldn't make it binding. I didn't realize until we were there, but I was familiar with the property. It's right next to the home James is building. I could see the construction site from the window of the minister's cabin. I hope this isn't one of Jokin' James's pranks."

"I don't think he's doing pranks anymore. I watch his videos, and it's mainly about the construction site. I think he has chickens now."

Hamish nodded, but I could tell he was concerned. And that caused a thought to wiggle its way into my head. "I kept cutting the minister off. He couldn't finish what he was saying. Maybe that's it."

"But he should have said something right then. Not a week and a half later when you're no longer a virgin."

I sat up, placing the coffee back on the table. I couldn't look at him. I had screwed up. Getting the inheritance was important to Hamish, and I already messed up his chances.

I was so focused on getting the ceremony over with that I never thought it might be important for the minister to say what he needed to say.

"Oh no… your inheritance."

He reached over, placing his hand on mine. His touch was warm and soothing. I hadn't needed Nancy in days; it was like Hamish was my new Nancy.

But despite his normally reassuring touch, I couldn't help but worry.

"Don't concern yourself about it. Jenner will make sure everything is fine. I followed my grandfather's directions. If the minister screwed up, then that's not our fault. The paperwork has been filed, and that's what's important."

But paperwork can get rejected. I lost count over how many times my parents' claims to their health insurance for my occupational therapy got rejected. It could easily happen, even to billionaires.

Once again, my selfish wants got in the way. I put my nephew at risk over two weeks ago, and now Hamish might lose his money.

I glanced up at him. He was staring out over the back gardens, lost in thought. I knew what he was thinking. He was wondering how he could screw up and marry someone like me.

All I had to do was marry him. It didn't take someone with an advanced degree to make that happen. And yet, I messed it up.

"Let's go for a walk around the estate. That will help clear our minds. I'm sure it was something tiny like the minister didn't initial something." Hamish smiled down at me.

But I noticed how his grin never met his eyes.
He wasn't happy. And it was all my fault.

Chapter Twenty-One

HAMISH

Jami had been quiet since we left the chalet.

I was worried about her. Every time I brought up the wedding or the minister, she winced.

And it wasn't just her face. The woman's entire body physically flinched when I talked about that day.

Did she regret marrying me?

They say the honeymoon period of a marriage doesn't last forever. Maybe it ended for Jami.

It's not as if she's in love with me.

Shit, that hurt. Just thinking about it sent a jolt of pain to my heart.

I was stupid to believe I could marry and not fall for her. It was time I admitted the truth: I was so far gone in love with Jami that I had no hope of coming back.

The marriage was a sham. She saw me as a fun guy to teach her about sex, but nothing more. And now that there were legal complications popping up, she was having second thoughts.

"Is anything wrong?" I asked, unable to take the silence much longer.

We strolled down a path close the edge of my property. On the other side of a swath of pine trees was the road. We were walking farther down, close to James Diaz's property. She said she watched his VidTube show, so I thought she might like to look over where he planned to live.

"I don't think I make a good wife."

I was right.

"What are you talking about? I couldn't imagine a better wife than you. You're beautiful, sexy, smart—"

"I'm not smart at all," she said, more to herself than me.

"Of course you are. When we do our cooking lessons, you always know how to convert ounces into cups. We didn't even need to look it up."

"Those are just facts. Facts can be memorized. That doesn't make someone smart."

I placed my hand on her back, and for the first time since I met her, she stiffened. Jami didn't want me to touch her.

I was losing her.

I stumbled to a stop, unable to go any farther. I pressed my hand against where my chest ached. If it were any other moment on any other day, I'd assume I was having a heart attack, but I knew better.

My heart wasn't beating too fast; it was breaking apart.

"Is this it, then?" My voice cracked. "Did I make a mistake choosing you to be my wife?"

Was that harsh? Yes. But I was hurt and angry, and rational thought was the last thing I was capable of.

Jami stopped, her shoulders slouched. She had her back to me, but I could tell my words hit their mark.

"It sure looks like you did," she said without turning around.

No. No, I didn't believe that. I shook my head and turned away from her toward the trees. I saw small snippets of beige from the dirt road on the other side of the trees. It was quiet, except for the birds singing their songs.

I pressed my fist to my lips. My body trembled as all I wanted to do was scream.

My grandfather was a terrible man. Maybe he didn't love me. That was all this was… a way to hurt me like he did everyone else. He knew the best way to break me was to make me give my heart to a woman who never wanted it in the first place.

I heard the leaves crunch and didn't bother to look back. I knew Jami was walking away. *Good.*

Maybe that was what we needed. Some cooling off away from each other.

Once I spent some time away from her, I'd see I was never in love with her. She was a good fuck, nothing more.

I heard some screeching and looked up. The dirt road filled with large black SUVs. People dressed in black came running through the trees toward me with guns in their hands.

"Hey, you can't be here. This is private property," I yelled over to them.

But they didn't hesitate. Turning, I saw another SUV drive over the grass of my estate and stop right in front of me.

The door opened, and a woman stepped out. I recognized her immediately, and my jaw dropped.

"Hamish Theodore Maximilian Blackwell," Katherine Alejandro said as she strolled up to me wearing black heels and a dark suit.

"Yes. But this is private property—"

She lifted her hand and held up a piece of paper. "We have a warrant, and I think you know why."

Damn it. I glanced back to see if Jami was okay, but she was gone. Did they arrest her too? Why would they? She never did anything wrong.

No, Jami must have run away once she saw what was happening.

As the men in black moved out of the trees, one of them came up to me and pulled my hands behind my back while another read me my rights.

It all felt like slow motion. Several weeks ago I was arrested, and I thought it was a joke.

This time was different. Loneliness consumed me as I realized my world was about to end, and the woman I loved wanted nothing to do with me.

Chapter Twenty-Two

JAMI

"I hear sirens," I mumbled as I moved up the hill to get a better look.

I saw black cars with flashing lights as they raced down the road, but soon the sirens stopped. It wasn't easy to get a clear view of the road from here.

It hurt when Hamish admitted he made a mistake marrying me, but it was the truth. I couldn't fault him for that; after all, it was the first thing I liked about him.

He told me the truth about my cranberry sauce.

I shook my head. I was stupid. Rock told me that was just how Hamish was, and it didn't matter who you were. He was brutally honest.

Now I understood when my sister told me sometimes the truth hurts. I thought life would be so much better if everyone was just honest with each other.

Life wasn't better with total honesty… It was only more painful.

But did I want him to lie? Did I want him to tell me he loved me like I loved him?

Because that was what was in my heart. Love. It wasn't just lust. It was everything. The sound of his voice in the morning when he whispered in my ear each day, "Rise and shine, my sleeping angel."

It was the way he smiled when I spouted out a random fact that related to what we were discussing. And despite how I felt right now, it was his honesty with me. He told me I was wrong when I needed to hear it.

I heard yelling, and it slapped me out of my self-pity. Running down the hill, I made my way through the trees and came out right when I saw Hamish being pushed into a black car.

"Hamish!" I cried out, but no one turned. I was too far away.

What was happening?

I gasped as I took off, trying to catch the car before it left. But I was only halfway through the field when the car turned. Even the cars on the road began to disperse.

When I finally made it to where Hamish had been, everyone was gone. *Who were in those cars?*

Did Hamish get arrested again? Maybe that DA woman found him. I had to reach out to Jenner and explain what happened.

I ran as quick as I could back to the chalet. I made my way through the hallways until I pushed open the door to our bedroom. I scanned the room to find my phone.

But as I looked, I realized I didn't have Jenner's number. Maybe Rock did. I kept up the hunt until my eyes landed on something better than my phone.

Hamish's phone.

I picked it up and typed in his password. My sister always hated that I could memorize their passwords just by looking at the movement of their fingers. Julia told me I had the calling of a cat burglar.

When I opened the text app, I found the text Jenner had sent earlier. That was where Jenner was, at the minister's house. I replied I was on my way and tucked his phone into my jeans pocket.

I ran outside and found the driver—the same guy who drove us here on our wedding day.

"Do you need to be driven somewhere, Ms. Blackwell?"

"My last name is Nutters—"

I was Ms. Blackwell. It was strange to be called by a new name. A nice kind of strange.

"I mean, yes, I do. Do you remember how to get back to the minister's cabin where Hamish and I were married?"

"I wouldn't be a very good driver if I didn't." He opened the door to the backseat and said, "Hop in. I'll have you there in no time."

I walked over but stopped right before I stepped inside. "I don't know your name. My name is Jami."

He bowed his head to me and said, "Paul. Paul Misk."

"Nice to meet you, Paul Misk."

His stern face softened when he smiled. Paul was tall with close-cropped red hair.

I slipped into the car, and Paul shut the door. It didn't take long before the car was moving. I watched through the window as the trees whipped past.

My heart pounded in my chest. I hoped Jenner could help Hamish.

I didn't wait for Paul to open the door when the car finally came to a stop. I bolted out.

"I'll be here by the vehicle when you need me," Paul called out as I raced to the door of the cabin.

I lifted my fist to knock, but the door swung open before I had a chance. It was the minister.

"Is Jenner here?" I tried to glance past him, but he filled the doorway.

He narrowed his eyes at me. "The person you want is out back." Then he slammed the door.

Ugh, why was Jenner out back? The minister must have kicked him out. He didn't come across as very hospitable.

I marched around the cabin and looked around. There was a field filled with rocks and patches of grass. Farther down the way was a tree line.

"Jenner?" I called out when I didn't see him.

I lifted my hand to shade my eyes. The sun was bright today. There was something moving near the trees, so I took several steps closer. That was when I saw someone waving their hand at me.

Even though he was in the shade, and it was difficult to get a good look at him, I started to jog toward him.

"Jenner, I'm coming. Something happened to Hamish," I yelled.

I was out of breath by the time I got near the tree line. I hunched over, placing my hands on my knees. As I gulped air, I heard footsteps inch closer. When I glanced up, I gasped.

I expected to see Jenner, but the person standing there sent an ice-cold shiver down my back. The moment I stood straight and tried to back away, Dick's hand snaked out and grabbed me.

His grip was strong. The more I struggled, the tighter he held on, to the point where his nails dug into my skin.

"What are you doing here? Where's Jenner?"

I kept trying to pull away, but I glanced back in hopes that Jenner was nearby. There was no one, not even the minister.

"I suspect he's at the police station trying to help my cousin."

"But he told Hamish to meet him here," I said more to myself than Dick.

Dick grinned, and it was the most unpleasant thing I had ever witnessed, like a creepy clown smile but without the makeup.

"No, Jenner didn't tell Hamish to meet him here." He reached into his black wool coat pocket and pulled out a phone. "I told Hamish to meet Jenner here. When I found Jenner's phone at Blue Bean, I knew it would come in handy, and it totally has."

"You? Why would you want Hamish here?"

He pulled me farther into the woods. At first, I continued my efforts to escape, but soon I accepted that his grip was too tight. My only chance was for him to loosen it. For any hope of that happening, I had to go along with him and make him think I gave up.

I walked alongside Dick through the brush and pine needles as we weaved our way into the woods. I noticed a clearing up ahead, and farther in the distance, it looked like a truck. Once I broke free, I could get to the truck.

My heart sank the closer we got. What if that was his truck?

Was he taking me there?

I looked around, and my hopes died. There was nowhere to go. If I went back the way we came, I doubted I would be fast enough to make it very far. Out here, in the mountains, houses were few and far between. And if I ran randomly into the woods, I'd get lost.

"I wanted Hamish here to kill him."

I came to a stop as my blood ran cold. He gave me a tough yank, and I stumbled forward.

"But he's your family."

Dick shrugged as we trudged forward. "Fuck family. My parents never cared about me. I'd only see them on major holidays and only for the purpose of parading me around for their friends. They wanted to show off what lovely parents they were, when in reality, it was all just a show. Look pretty, act pretty, you must be a wonderful person. What a joke."

I watched his hard stare as he focused on moving forward. A part of me felt sorry for Dick as a child. A kid who only wanted love and attention and got nothing.

"I'm sorry."

His head whipped around, and he glared at me. "Don't be. I took care of them. Suddenly, as they aged, they needed me. Too late. I gave them as much attention as they gave me. In the end, it turned out that didn't make for a nurturing environment."

My stomach turned. What had he done to his parents? I felt sick. I cupped my mouth. "Oh god."

"My parents are in the past. It's time to think of the future. A future where I get my grandfather's inheritance."

"But Hamish is married to me."

Once we broke the tree line, I saw it wasn't a truck in the distance; it was actually a bulldozer. Looking around, I saw lots of construction equipment and materials. Something about the place seemed familiar, but I just couldn't figure out why.

"Hamish thought he married you. Once I found out you were his fiancée, I did a little digging. Unfortunately, you were the perfect bride. A virgin. The right age. There was nothing I could use from your past to nullify the marriage. That's when I had to get creative. So I paid Henry to marry you."

We finally came to a stop by a large hole.

"Henry? Who's Henry?"

"The minister." He gave me a look that was all too familiar. There were a lot of people growing up who gave that expression when they thought I was too stupid to understand. "I paid him to pretend to be a minister. He was one of those tinfoil hat nutters… Sorry." Dick snickered.

My lips thinned as I waited for him to continue.

"Anyway, he was crazy and just religious enough to take the bait when I called you sinners who needed healing. That you two needed to think you were married to each other so I could perform my final right to cast the demons out of you, or something to that effect. He ate it all up."

"That's why he said we were sinners and didn't want us kissing in his house." That weirdly made sense.

Dick shook his head. "God, that guy was nuts, but he served a purpose. You two were married by a phony, and the way you kissed him after the ceremony, I can only assume you aren't a virgin anymore."

My eyes widened as his words hit me like a fist to my gut.

Hamish can't get the inheritance now, and all the money will go to Dick.

Chapter Twenty-Three

HAMISH

I sat in a small room with a mirror on one wall. I'd seen enough cop shows to know this was the interrogation room. Thankfully, when the cops led me in here, they took off the handcuffs.

They had left me alone for quite a while. I had no idea the time, as there was no clock in here.

I missed Jami. She probably thought I left her out there on the property. Maybe that made her happy.

This was the perfect opportunity for her to be free of me. I was going to jail for murder, and there was nothing I could do about it. I doubt even Jenner could fight the DA. I bet the DA requested that no bail be set for me from the judge.

I had seen that once on a show, so I figured it was a thing.

Even if Jenner was right outside that door, fighting for me to be set free, I didn't care. Rock and Monty and all the Diaz brothers could be there, and it didn't matter.

The only person I wanted right now was Jami. But she was gone, and I doubted I'd ever see her again.

The door opened.

Katherine Alejandro stood there, her dark hair pulled back in a tight bun. Wordlessly, she moved to the table and slid into the chair across from me.

She placed one manila folder on the table in front of her. "Do you know what's in this folder, Mr. Blackwell?" She tapped the folder with a red-manicured nail.

"I guess it's about me?"

She shook her head. "Try again."

My jaw tightened. I really wasn't in the mood to play games.

"The victim, Tiberius Endicott."

Her head tilted, and not a hair on her head moved. "Nope, but I'll let you have one more guess since I'm feeling frisky today."

I rubbed the back of my neck. "I don't know. Santa Claus?"

For fuck's sake, she thought me being charged with murder was a joke. I guess ruining an innocent person's life was fun for her.

"Wrong again. And if it was about Santa Claus, my kids would never speak to me again."

She was someone's mother? Damn, I felt sorry for those kids.

I sat back and folded my arms. "Can we get on with this please? This has been a pretty shitty day, and if I'm honest, being arrested wasn't the worst part."

Her satisfied grin faltered. She let out a breath and opened the folder, then turned it toward me. "Does this man look familiar to you, Mr. Blackwell?"

I gazed down at the smiling man. His face was weathered; his dark eyes matched his dark hair, probably in his forties, but it appeared he'd spent some time in the sun—either that or life just hadn't been good to him. It looked like a work photo. Maybe something needed for ID. Maybe even a driver's license picture.

I shook my head. "No. Who's that?"

"That is Tiberius Endicott. We found his body in your home, stuffed in one of your bedroom closets, three weeks ago. Actually, it was your maid who found the body."

I sat up as my heart pounded in my throat. "I don't know him. I have no idea how he got into my home." My mind raced with possibilities of who could have done this. "My servants had access to the penthouse. It could have been any number of people."

She sat there, taking in everything I had to say. "You're right, Hamish. Is it okay if I call you Hamish?"

No, but I suspected she didn't care what I said. This was her way of controlling me.

"While your prints are all over the home—as would be expected—they aren't on the body. There's a statue that was found right by the body with your prints on it. And since Tiberius's head had wounds consistent with blunt-force trauma, the police came to the conclusion that you killed him."

"Why would I do that? Even if I knew the man, which I don't, why would I kill him?"

She nodded and leaned forward. "That's the part I keep getting stuck on. *Why*? Why him?"

I stared at her, waiting for her to finish but, apparently, she was.

"How the hell should I know? As I told every police officer since I found out about the murder, I have never met Tiberius Endicott." I slammed my fist against the table.

I was ready to pick up the table and throw it against the wall, but I was pretty sure that would make this situation worse.

The corner of her mouth ticked up. She was getting off on my frustration. I guess the more twisted and fucked-up you were, the easier it was to be the district attorney.

"Look, Hamish, it's time to be straight with you. While all signs pointed to you murdering Tiberius, after the last of the autopsy results came back today—the bloodwork—it seemed the victim wasn't killed by blunt-force trauma. He overdosed on heroin."

My head jerked back. "He overdosed? Then why the fuck am I here?"

"Because I still believe the man was killed. Just because someone overdosed on a drug doesn't mean they were a drug addict. In fact, when my detectives met with his family and friends, not one of them ever said he had a drug problem. And heroin addiction is a hard addiction to hide. His friends said he never did drugs and rarely drank. And when he did drink, it was just a few beers at a cookout or a party. He had a live-in girlfriend, and she saw no evidence of addiction to anything.

"He worked construction, so there was lots of physical labor. If he had a bad heroin problem, I doubt he would be any good at his job. His boss loved him. He told us

Tiberius was his best employee. He was always on time and never missed work. Hard worker. The whole nine yards. Nothing about his death makes sense to me. That's why you're here."

I felt like scratching off my face; I was incredibly frustrated.

"So, you think because he wasn't an addict, I must have given him heroin? Some random construction worker."

She shook her head. "Not you. Your cousin, Dickinson Kerry."

My body stiffened.

"Then why did you arrest me? Did you drop the charges against me? If so, that means I'm free to go. Since you want Dick and not me."

I started to get up before she said, "Wait. We had new evidence and at the time of your arrest, I believed you were the murderer. But in the time we've come back here, I've received new information. You may not agree, but maybe it was a good thing we arrested you."

My brow arched. "Really?"

"Yes. We now believe Dickinson Kerry killed Tiberius Endicott. I've sent a few officers to The Blue Spot to arrest your cousin but he's not there. We think he may be spying on you. If he thinks you've been arrested, then in his eyes, he's safe. We are hoping he'll return to his room at the resort so we can arrest him."

I nodded, sitting back and waved for her to continue.

"We believe Tiberius witnessed something. His girlfriend told us he was doing some drywall work on the side, and it took us a while to find out where he was doing the work. Since it was a side project he was doing outside of his job, there wasn't any paperwork. It took us a few weeks to find out he was hired by Mr. Kerry to do some work on his pool house."

She shifted the papers in the folder, pulling out a crumpled note. "His girlfriend managed to find this under their bed yesterday. It's your cousin's address. When we went there this morning, the butler told us Tiberius had been hired to do work on the property. His girlfriend told us that the day before he went missing, Tiberius came home very upset… scared. He said he saw something terrible, but he wouldn't tell her what it was. Just that he was going the next day to pick up his tools and quit. He didn't want anything to do with the guy who hired him.

"But he never came home the next day. His girlfriend filed a missing person report, and the next day, your maid found his body in your home. We assumed you hired him to do work and became angry when he quit. Now we know different."

I leaned forward, placing my elbows on the table, trying to make sense of the DA's words. *What did Tiberius see?*

"Then why aren't you out there looking for Dick? You checked his room but that's it."

"We are looking all over town. I wish it were that easy to locate criminals, but it isn't." She smirked.

"That's why I wanted to explain everything to you before you left. If you see him or know where he might be, please let us know. You might be in danger too. The blow to Tiberius's head was done after he died. We believe Dick planted the body in your home to frame you. If he finds out you aren't being arrested he might come after you."

She took a breath before she continued, "If Dick caught him witnessing something, then Dick wouldn't want that getting out. He now had a reason to get rid of Tiberius."

"And stage it to look like I did it. My grandfather recently passed," I mumbled.

"I am sorry for your loss."

Don't be. Grandfather would have called this woman every derogatory name in the book, but she didn't need to know that. With all I had been through over the past several weeks, I was realizing that maybe my grandfather wasn't worth the hoops I was jumping through for him.

"I appreciate the sentiment, but he wasn't a nice guy. Maybe that's why he hated Dick. He saw all that was wrong in himself in my cousin."

Maybe family wasn't made from blood, but from love.

"In my grandfather's will, he left everything to me on certain conditions, and Dick got nothing. But if I didn't adhere to those conditions, then everything went to Dick. I think he framed me to get rid of me."

"That could be it." She tapped her red lip with her nail.

"But even if I get thrown in jail for years, I still get the inheritance. That won't stop it from happening."

There was yelling outside the door, and we both looked up as it opened.

I was shocked to find James Diaz standing there next to Jenner and an officer.

"I'm sorry, ma'am, but these two insisted on—"

"You are not holding my client here on any charges. He is free to go." Jenner pointed at the DA.

Katherine held up her hands. "He's right. Hamish is free to go."

"Great. Then we can head over to my place?" James asked.

I shook my head as I stood. "No. What makes you think I want to hang out at your place? I told you I will never be in one of your videos."

James reached into his pocket and pulled out his phone. After a few taps, he held it up. "That's too bad, Hamish... because your wife is on the current one."

I grabbed the phone from him. There was a video of Jami standing in a hole while dirt was being tossed on her. I couldn't make out who was throwing the dirt because they were off camera.

"Why is she there? Did you put her up to this, James?"

He shook his head. "I don't know anything about it. My phone pinged me about a half hour ago that there was movement on my property. I have cameras everywhere on that land. It's my job to film things for entertainment. I like to use real footage of animals on my property, so the moment there's movement, they start recording. I checked what the cameras were filming, thinking it would be a deer or squirrel, but then I saw Jami."

I rubbed my forehead. "She said she watched your show. Oh shit. Our fight. Maybe she had Paul drive her there to find you?"

I bet she wanted to get away from me as soon as possible.

"But why would she leave the house? I told her, and you, not to leave," Jenner said.

"Not this morning. You texted me that we needed to meet at the minister's place because something went wrong with the ceremony."

Jenner's brows lowered. "No, I didn't. I haven't texted you all day."

I instinctively reached for my back pocket and realized my phone wasn't there. That was when something came to me.

"Did you lose your phone recently, Jenner?"

He rubbed the back of his neck. "Yes. Yesterday."

"Where?"

"I think at Blue Beans, but when I went back, they didn't have it."

I let out a sigh.

Jenner and I both blurted out at the same time, "Dick."

Chapter Twenty-Four

JAMI

As much as I tried, I couldn't climb out of the hole Dick had pushed me into. It was deeper than I thought, and the soil was too wet from the rain yesterday. Every time I started to make progress, I slid right back down.

"Why do you even bother? Accept your fate, Jami. You weren't married into wealth. Look at you. You're just a dirty, stupid girl who only got into college because the university had to meet a quota. They needed a certain number of people with disabilities to get government funding. You do realize the whole world runs on money. If they had no funding, then people like you could never get a diploma. And once I get my inheritance, I'll pay off so many politicians to make sure dummies like you stay out of society."

"I actually got a scholarship," I mumbled.

He put down the shovel and clapped. "Good for you. You beat out other dummies to get money for school. Thus, proving my point that it's all because of money."

"Actually, I beat out a bunch of neurotypicals to get that scholarship."

Even from here, I could tell I upset him.

"It doesn't matter. You'll be dead, and life will move on. Even Hamish will be thanking me that I got rid of his dopey girlfriend."

My nostrils flared. I hated that he was right. My death would be another problem solved for Hamish. He may not get the money, but he wouldn't have to deal with me anymore.

Hot tears streamed down my face.

Screw men. I hated them all. The only man who ever treated me with respect was my father. I wished he was here to help me.

"Aw, I'm so sorry the truth hurts, but you needed to learn someday, even if it's your last day on Earth, that you can't rely on anyone for love. You can only rely on yourself."

"I hate you."

"Join the club." He laughed as he threw a shovel of dirt on me again.

"I can't even depend on people I hire." He shook his head. "Take Tiberius Endicott, for instance. Great name, by the way, but wasted on a construction worker." He stuck out his tongue like he was about to throw up.

"What about him?"

How did Dick know Tiberius was a construction worker?

"I hired him to add some walls in my pool house, and the guy went nosing around where he had no business being. He found a small basement storage room in the pool house. Most people don't know about it because there's a trapdoor hidden under a Persian rug. It's where I keep expensive wines… and my parents."

My head went back. "Your parents? I thought they were dead?"

When we were walking through the woods, Dick made it seem that they had died. Had I misheard him?

"Oh, they are… but I couldn't let anyone find out *how* they died. I paid someone for two bodies to be in that accident. The car accident they were in wasn't an actual car accident, just made to look that way. It was two dead bodies so badly burned that they were unrecognizable. Thankfully, there were dental records. And let me tell you, pulling teeth from my parents' dead bodies to plant at the car accident wasn't easy. I worked my ass off for their money."

My mouth fell open.

He was a monster.

"And stupid Tiberius found them. Of course, I had to kill him too. But when I heard I got nothing from my grandfather, I thought I could kill two birds with one stone, pun intended. I'd make it look like Hamish killed him. Can I just say, security is so lax in New York City buildings nowadays. It was easy to dress up as a maintenance worker and haul a body into Hamish's building. He really should consider moving."

I could barely believe what I was hearing.

"Then he met you, so I had to make sure you two weren't actually married. And that brings us here. I had planned to bury Hamish alive, but you showed up instead."

Adrenaline raced through my body. I didn't want to be here. I wanted to turn back time and not fight with Hamish. I wanted to tell him that I loved him, even if he didn't love me.

If I had just been honest with him, then none of this would have happened.

"I'm sorry," I said as I wiped at my tears.

"Apology accepted."

"Not for you, jerk. I'm apologizing to Hamish." I raised my voice. "I know you can't hear me, Hamish, but I love you. I was too afraid to tell you... but I do. And I'd rather it was me being buried alive instead of you. I don't think I would be able feel love again without you. Wherever you are, I hope you are safe and loved. That's all I ever wanted for you."

Dick opened his mouth, but another man's words filled the air.

"I love you too, Jami."

I recognized Hamish's voice instantly. He was far off, but I heard him clearly.

Dick held up the shovel like a bat and quickly turned.

"Drop your weapon, Dickinson Kerry. You are under arrest," a woman shouted.

I stood on my tiptoes trying to catch a glimpse of what was going on, but all I could see was Dick dropping the shovel and raising his hands into the air. There was shouting, and Dick was pulled away. I screamed that I was in the hole, but no one came. The voices sounded as if they were growing distant.

Was everyone leaving?

"I'm down here!" I tried again, even as my voice was growing hoarse.

Stopping to listen, all I heard were birds chirping and some rustling leaves from the breeze. Hamish had been here, but he left.

"I can't believe he left me." I gazed down at the dirt that was pooled around my feet.

"I'd never leave you," Hamish said with his hands on his hips, peering over the edge of the hole.

Ease washed over me. I was safe, and he was here. I clasped my hand over my heart and said, "I meant what I said. I love you."

He nodded and turned before disappearing.

The smile on my face faltered. *Oh no, had I scared him off?*

"Hamish?" I called out, but there was no response.

I pulled at some strands of hair, causing dirt to tumble to the ground. Not only was I stuck here, but I had scared off the only man I ever loved.

I heard some clanking sounds, and then a long metal ladder was lowered into the hole. At the top, holding the ladder straight, was the man I loved.

"Can you climb up?"

I shook off the dirt on my shoes and grabbed the ladder, taking my first step. Once I was at the top, I wanted to throw my arms around Hamish, but I hesitated.

"I thought you left again. I thought I scared you off when I said I loved you."

He reached up and brushed more dirt from my cheek. "That only made me more determined to get you out. The police told me to wait until the medics showed up, but I wanted you by my side."

He stepped forward and pulled me in for a hug. His embrace was warm but gentle, and I sagged in his arms. All the stress of the past hour melted away as I leaned my head against his chest.

"I needed the woman I loved in my arms," he whispered into my ear.

My heart thundered in my chest. Hamish loved me. My lips curved into a silly grin.

"I'm really dirty. We probably shouldn't be touching," I said as I curled my fingers into the lapels of his jacket and held him tight.

"You're my wife; you're allowed to get me dirty." He wiggled his eyebrows. "In fact... I prefer it."

My smile faded, and I took a step back. "But we aren't married. Dick hired the minister and gave him a fake license. He never had the authority to marry us." I swallowed. "And that means you don't get your inheritance."

"God, Dick is such a dick," Hamish said as his jaw tightened.

"There's still time. You don't turn thirty until next week. Maybe I can find you a twenty-one-year-old virgin. That's initially what I was supposed to do... There's still time—"

He held his finger up to my lips. "No."

I pushed his hand away. "It's fine. I won't mind," I lied. It would eat me alive if I saw Hamish say *I do* to another woman, but I loved him. I'd do anything to make him happy, even let him go.

He smiled softly. "You're a terrible liar, Jami."

My eyes dipped to the ground. "I guess I'm just not used to it. So, I would mind, but it's important that Dick doesn't get that money. Even if he goes to jail, he will still get that money."

We stood there in silence as sirens rang in the distance.

After a minute, Hamish sighed. "Is that really important to you? To see me married?"

I nodded as my eyes filled with tears.

He slipped his arm over my shoulder, and he directed me away from the pit. "I only want to make you happy, Jami. If this is what it takes, then I'll marry."

I squeezed my eyes shut and nodded. I did my best to hold back the tears. Thankfully, Hamish was distracted by the ambulance that just pulled up as a few tears slipped down my face.

It was good the medics were here because my heart just broke.

Chapter Twenty-Five

HAMISH

Five days.

That was all it took to throw a wedding together. We found a proper justice of the peace. Someone who didn't live in a cabin in the woods or call people sinners.

Also, the location. Rock let us use The Blue Chip. The tables had been removed, and chairs were set in rows for guests. White and red roses were everywhere, even the wood molding on the walls were covered with ribbons hanging down, dotted with flowers.

I stood at the front with the justice of the peace, waiting for the ceremony to start. "This was a dumb idea." I turned to Jenner, who stood next to me as my best man.

He wore a dark gray suit with a white rose tucked into his lapel. I wore a dark navy suit with a gray vest and a red rose in my lapel. Even with the cold wind whipping outside, I was sweating.

"No, it wasn't. I never thought I'd say this, but you need to marry."

I shook my head. "But all the secrecy. I'm regretting it. Regretting everything. I should have told her."

I loved Jami with all my heart, but I felt sick keeping who the bride was from her. All she knew was I was getting married today.

"No, you shouldn't have." Jenner stepped closer, placing his hand on my shoulder. "Once the ceremony is done, we can move on. You'll get your inheritance, and you two can just be happy."

"Fuck the inheritance. I'm giving all of it away."

Jenner chuckled. "Not all of it." His laughter slowly faded. "No, seriously, Hamish. You aren't actually giving all the money away, are you?"

I turned to my best man. "Yes. I don't need it. If I did nothing with my life and lived off the money I already have for the rest of my life, I'd still have plenty left over. At least tens of millions. I could live to a hundred and be fine."

I checked the double doors that led to the hallway. Jami wasn't here, and I wondered if she'd show up at all.

Everyone was in on it; even her sisters knew Jami was to be my bride. There was no one else I'd ever consider marrying.

But with Jami not here, I wondered if she refused to come.

"As your lawyer, I'd advise you to keep at least some of your grandfather's money for—"

"You aren't my financial planner or my accountant. As a lawyer, you have no say in what I do with my money, only that I get it. By the end of the day, it will all be transferred over to me."

Jenner rubbed his brow.

Why was I getting the money today? It wasn't because I was marrying. It was because today was the day Dick was being charged with tax fraud—the one thing in the will that would disqualify him. Which meant that the money went back to me.

The DA let me know all the charges Dick was facing. Since the jerk admitted everything to Jami the day he kidnapped her and James' cameras recorded it all. There's no judge or jury in the country that won't convict him by his own admission of guilt.

When the DA got to tax fraud, I literally jumped for joy.

"You told me several weeks ago that you met Dick's lawyer, and he hadn't committed tax fraud."

"Yeah, that lawyer was arrested too. He lied to me. Dick was committing lots of fraud and paying off his lawyer so he wouldn't go to the Feds. You may not know this, Hamish, but there are some crooked lawyers out there," Jenner said.

I threw my head back and laughed. I needed a good chuckle.

"I'm serious, Hamish. They aren't all good like me."

My god, Jenner was serious. He really thought I'd be surprised at his revelation.

The soft, classical music that played over the speakers changed to the Wedding March. I glanced toward the door to see Jami standing there in an emerald-green velvet gown that was ruched in the front. Her hair was pulled into a thick braid that trailed down her back. My nostril flared as I reveled in her beauty.

She held a small bouquet of red and white roses. And this time, the flowers were real. Once she got to the front, she moved off to the side of the justice, never looking at me.

"Let's start the ceremony, shall we?" The justice of the peace stood, his thick gray hair flopping in front of his eyes.

Jami glanced around the room before turning back to him. "But what about the bride? She isn't here."

I smiled and took a step forward, getting down on one knee and gazed up into her sparkling brown eyes. "Jami Nutters, would you make me the happiest man in the world and agree to marry me? Not only that, but marry me today, in front of all these people."

I reached into my pocket and pulled out a black velvet box. Opening it, I plucked out the two-carat yellow diamond ring.

She gasped, bringing her hand to her mouth. "But," she lowered her hand and shook her head, "you have to marry a virgin. I'm not a virgin, remember?"

I heard a few chuckles from the crowd but ignored them.

"No, I don't. Dick won't be getting the inheritance. He's been charged with fraud, along with murder and lots of other crimes. That makes my grandfather's money automatically go to me, whether I'm married or not."

That cute little wrinkle appeared between her eyes. "But that means you don't have to get married. Why are you going through with this?"

"Because I love you. And the past several weeks made me realize that before I met you, my life was boring. I traveled the world, visited estates and resorts, and went to outrageous parties, but at the end of it all, I was alone. Not just physically alone, but my heart was empty."

I took a deep breath, hoping my voice didn't wobble, and continued, "When you smiled, I felt a little warmer. When you held my hand, I was a little stronger. And when you spoke to me, I became a whole lot wiser. You helped me see the beauty of everything around me, that it couldn't be bought. Now I hope you take my hand and never let go."

Her hands slipped over mine, and she nodded. "Yes. I'll never let go."

Everyone clapped as I stood and slipped the engagement ring onto her finger.

We hugged and kissed, and when I stepped back, I noticed her fiddling with the ring.

"Doesn't it fit?"

"Yes, it does. I'm just not used to wearing rings. It's unusual." She slipped her hand into mine as we turned to face the justice of the peace.

"I like unusual. That's been our entire relationship. And after this is over, I plan to show you just how much fun *unusual* can be."

I cupped her cheeks and slipped my lips over hers. I wanted to savor every moment with the woman I loved. No cutting off the justice of the peace this time. I would stand by her side and hold her hand, no matter how long it took. She was going to be my wife, and I never wanted it any other way.

• • • • • • • • • •

The End

Blue Ridge Mountain Billionaires Series Order

About The Author

Elizabeth Lynx is a USA Today Bestselling author that writes rom-coms with a lot of steam and characters that cause you to laugh-out-loud. She has worn many hats in life: mother, wife, photographer, graphic designer, executive assistant, and used to print pictures for the White House. For the past several years, she's put down on paper all the crazy voices in her head. Those voices have done some naughty things.

Find out more about Elizabeth on her website: www.elizabeth-lynx.com

Feel free to reach out to her via email at lynxelizabeth1@gmail.com